HOUSE GUEST

HOUSE GUEST

J Chambers

Library of Congress Control Number:		2019915161
ISBN:	Hardcover	978-1-7960-6252-6
	Softcover	978-1-7960-6251-9
	eBook	978-1-7960-6250-2

To order additional copies of this book, contact:
Xlibris
1-888-795-4274
www.Xlibris.com
Orders@Xlibris.com
800678

PART 1

Robert McKinley is the owner and founder of McKinley Hardware Store. He has a wife named Sarah McKinley and two little girls named Mikaela, who is twelve years old, and Caitlin, who is ten years old.

Robert was working in the store one day. A gentleman came into the store looking for a few items to hang some pictures and to get some yellow sticky pads and a few more items. This guy caught Robert's attention for one reason: he looked confused as he looked for what he needed, but eventually, he found what he wanted and proceeded to get in line to pay for them.

When he became the next person in line, Robert said, "Hi, sir, did you find everything you needed today?"

The gentleman took his hand to his face and massaged it as if he had a beard and answered Robert hesitantly, "Yes, I did, thank you."

Robert went on to say as he was ringing up the man's items. "It's a nice day out."

The gentleman said, "Ah, yeah, it is."

Robert caught on to the way he said it as if he had something more to say. So Robert smiled softly and said, "But . . ." Like to have finish his sentence.

The guy smiled back and said, "Well, no, I'm just trying to get a job and, you know, keep things being productive in my life."

Robert said with sympathy, "Oh yeah, I understand, man." Robert was saying to himself, *Seems like he just got out of jail, just trying to do the right thing.*

Robert told him the price of his items, and the guy paid Robert his total amount. As Robert was putting the items in the bag, he asked the guy, "Are you looking for a job?"

The guy nodded his head up and down slowly, responding, "Yes, I am."

Robert ripped a quick piece of paper off the register roll and wrote his phone number down and handed it to the guy. As the guy held his hand out to take it, Robert said, "Give me a call. I think I might be able to help you."

The guy looked up at Robert as though he heard his name called for the first time, listening to each word coming out of Robert's mouth. The guy responded, "Sure."

Robert said, "This evening, around seven."

The guy was so happy and excited and felt that things were starting to look good for him. Robert gave him the bag with the things he paid for. The guy took the bag and said, "Thank you, and I will."

Robert smiled back and said immediately, "Oh, my name is Robert."

The guy shook Robert's hand and smiled back. "My name is Jazz." Jazz said, "Thanks again," and proceeded to leave the store

Robert proceeded to ring up the next customer who just got in line to have their items rung up.

Robert turned to look at Jazz as he walked by the store window.

As the day became evening, Robert closed up the shop. He was feeling good after a good day at the store.

He drove home and walked up the brick pathway to his front door. He put his key in the door, yelling,

"Daddy's home!" Caitlin and Mikaela ran down the stairs with excitement, screaming, "Hi, Daddy!" Caitlin grabbed his thigh because of his height, and Mikaela grabbed his waist because she is a little taller than Caitlin.

Sarah came down stairs soon after and said, "Come on, girls. Let Daddy go so he can clean up for dinner."

Robert continued to his bedroom to clean up and to get ready for dinner. Sarah walked to the kitchen to put the food on the table. She called the girls to come eat dinner. Robert heard her as well. They all were sitting at the table, and Robert asked Mikaela, "Mikaela, how was school today?"

Mikaela said, "Daddy, it was fun today. We went outside. We played kickball"

Robert smiled as he watched her eating, admiring how much she looked like him. He asked her, "Did you win?"

She said, "Yes, it was the boys against the girls." She went on to say, "We always beat boys," and smiled at her daddy.

Robert went on to say, "How was Princess Caitlin's day at school today?".

Caitlin giggled back at her father. She said, "Daddy, it was good. I drew you and Mommy a picture."

Sarah and Robert looked at each other and then looked back at her and said, "Oh really?" They said it together almost in stereo.

Caitlin said, "Yep." Caitlin immediately added, "But I didn't get to finish it today."

Sadly, Sarah said, "That's OK, princess."

Caitlin said, "I will finish it tomorrow."

Robert said, "I can't wait to see it." He smiled back at her and Sarah and said, "And you, the queen of my two little princesses?"

The girls started to laugh, and Sarah look at Robert. He went on to say, "And how was your day?"

Sarah said, "It was nice and quiet. I like it like that." She smiled at Robert.

"Well," said Robert, "I had a pretty interesting day."

Sarah replied, "Oh."

He went on to say, "This gentleman came into the store. He was looking for a few items. I think I'm going to offer him a job."

Sarah said, "He's not working?"

Robert said, "I don't think so. I gave him my phone number for him to call me tonight around, seven."

Sarah said,

"That was an interesting day for you."

Robert smiled.

PART 2

Ironically, as they were finishing up dinner, the phone rang. Robert walked over and picked up the phone. Robert said, "Hello."

It was Jazz. He called just like Robert told him to. He said, "Hello. May I please speak to Robert?"

Robert excitedly said, "This is he."

Jazz went on to say, "This is Jazz, the guy that was in your store today that talked to you briefly."

Robert excitedly said, "Yes! I remember." Robert dominated the next sentence he said. "So I know you mentioned earlier in the store you didn't have a job and you were looking for one, correct?"

Jazz said, "That's correct. It's so hard to get employment now."

Robert could feel Jazz had been in trouble before and didn't want him to lose confidence. Robert quickly said, "I can imagine." He went on to say, "I have a position in the store as a stock person and would like to hire you if you want the job."

Jazz said, "So you are offering me a job?" Smiling throughout the question he just asked Robert.

Robert said, "Yes, you would have to fill out the application and W-2 form. But yes, I'm offering you a job."

Jazz was so happy. This was what he had been waiting for. He had been trying so hard for employment.

Jazz said to Robert, "Yes! I will take the job."

Robert said, "Great! Please be at the store 8:00 a.m. sharp, and I will get you started with the inventory list. The store hours are 8:30 a.m. to 6:00 p.m."

After Robert had mentioned the store hours, Jazz said to Robert, "I have a slight problem."

Robert said, "What is it?"

Jazz said, "Where I live at, I must be in the house by 5:30 p.m."

Robert said, "Oh I see." He was now convinced that Jazz was trying to get back into society. He said, "Can I call you back in a couple of minutes?"

Jazz said in kind of a sad voice, "Sure."

Robert said, "OK, great."

When they hung up, he walked up the stairs to the bedroom where his wife was. She was looking over Mikaela and Caitlin's homeworks. She looked up over the glasses she was wearing. She saw Robert at the door staring at her like a little kid who has a question for her.

Sarah said, "Is there a problem?"

Robert said, "Well, yes." He went on to say, "Jazz—you know the guy I'm hiring?"

She said, "Yeah?"

Robert went on to say, "He has a curfew where he lives."

Sarah said, "OK," as if she was trying to tell Robert to get to the point.

Robert said. "Well, we got another bedroom—the guestroom down the hall. I was thinking he could stay there, pay room and board for his own dependence, and things should be fine".

Sarah said. "I don't know. You seem to have a heavy liking to this guy."

Robert said, "I just want to see him succeed."

Sarah said, "If you're OK with it, then I will trust your instincts."

Robert put on a big smile and ran back downstairs like a kid waking up on Christmas Day looking for toys. He proceeded to call Jazz back on the phone.

The phone rang on Jazz's end twice. Jazz picked up the phone he said, "Hello?"

Robert went on to say, "May I speak to Jazz please?"

Jazz said, "This is he."

Robert said, "This is Robert from the hardware store."

Jazz said, "Yes, I know."

Robert said, "I would like to offer you a room in the house where I stay. And you can pay room and board just like an apartment through the checks you get by working."

Jazz said in a happy voice, "So you're offering me a job and a place?"

Robert said, "Yes, I am."

Jazz said loudly with laughter, "Yes. Yes, I'll take it! Thank you!"

Robert was smiling on the other end of the line. He quietly said on the other end of the line, "I will see you tomorrow. Have a nice evening." And then he hung up.

Part 3

So Robert did what he normally does in the store in the morning. It was around 8:00 a.m. Jazz strolled in about 7:50 a.m. Robert said good morning to Jazz and said, "I'll be right with you."

He walked near Jazz, and Jazz shook his hand and said, "Good morning."

Robert proceeded to show Jazz how he would like him to stock the shelves. Jazz caught on quickly, and Robert left him on his own doing his job.

The evening came quickly. Robert started to close the store. Jazz was excited to see the new place where he would be living. He had not had his own room in years. So now he and Robert arrived home. The house looked great in Jazz eyes. He was anticipating what his room looked like.

They walked up the walkway. Jazz was slightly behind Robert, who turned the key to enter the house, yelling, "Honey, I'm home!"

Sarah coming downstairs with Mikaela and Caitlin trailing her. She kissed Robert and said, "Hi, honey." The kids were hugging him at his waist, saying in a high voice tone, "Hi, Daddy!"

Jazz is taking this all in staring and saying to himself, *Wow!* as if he was part of the family. Robert paused and then said, "Sarah, Mikaela, Caitlin, this is Jazz."

The girls said, "Hi, Jazz!"

Sarah said after the girls, "Hi, Jazz."

Jazz responded to them all with only one word: "Hi." He felt that this was a beautiful moment. Robert told Jazz to follow him—he would show him his room and the rest of the house. Jazz walked behind Robert.

Robert showed Jazz the bathroom and walked up a few stairs and down the hallway to show him his bedroom. The door was open. Jazz saw his spacious room. King-sized bed and was well please. After taking it all in, he turned and looked at Robert and said humbly, "Thank you."

With a humble peaceful smile and with satisfaction, Robert turned and walked away to join his family. Robert yelled with his back turn saying, "Dinner in thirty minutes. Please join us?"

Jazz said, "OK."

PART 4

Jazz cleaned up a little. He came downstairs to join the family at dinner. They all sat down. The children said grace almost in unison. As they started eating, everyone glance around the table, with Sarah looking at Robert and smiling. She was thinking about how he get wrapped up in all his obligations and sometimes neglected her. He finally looked at Sarah; his eyes were showing signs he loved her very much.

Sarah asked Jazz, just to make him feel comfortable, where was he from, and did he have brothers and sisters?

Jazz answered quickly as he was eating. He said, "There's five of us—three girls and two boys. I'm the youngest." He said, "The food tastes great." He was just thinking not so long ago about how the food tasted when he was in jail.

Sarah said. "Thank you." She also said, "Does anyone want dessert?"

Robert and Jazz declined. Jazz humbly excused himself and went to his room. Mikaela and Caitlin did as well. The girls went to their room to play their electronic games before bedtime. Sarah began cleaning up the kitchen and washing the dishes. Robert joined her in cleaning the kitchen. He was drying the dishes.

Once the kitchen was clean, they both went to their bedroom to relax and go to bed. The evening went fast; morning came quickly. Sarah woke up first, mainly to make breakfast and to get Mikaela and Caitlin ready to go to school.

Robert knocked on Jazz's door to tell him about breakfast. Jazz came down to eat. They all were at the kitchen table once again. This time, they all ate rather quickly. Jazz and Robert hurried off to work once they finished their food. Sarah was moving quickly so she could drop the girls off at school. After dropping Mikaela and Caitlin off at school, Sarah drove off to work as well.

Robert and Jazz arrived at the store, and it was a smooth day for them both. Jazz conversed much more, talking to Robert about sports and current events, even with the customers, as they all laughed and chuckled when funny comments were made.

Sarah texted Robert throughout the day with love messages to never let him forget how much she loved him. The evening came quickly. They closed the store and headed home. They arrived at the house. Jazz was feeling more and more comfortable with his life and freedom since getting the job and having his place to stay without a curfew.

Life was becoming comfortable for all. Days turned into weeks, weeks turning into months. They became all so comfortable. Although Jazz would sometimes hear them arguing or having disagreements, ranging from attention she wanted from Robert or places he had promised to take her to. Jazz never held anything against him or her. He knew they were good people. He would eventually turn over and go to sleep.

As time went on, Robert would leave early to go work, since everyone was comfortable. Jazz would wake up, take a shower, and go in to work on his own and meet Robert at the store. He would punch in and out and do his job. Everything was working like a well-oiled machine. Jazz would be the last one leaving the house, or sometimes Sarah would be. Robert was always the first one out of the house, like a race dog out of the gate.

PART 5

These days, everything and everyone had their routine down. Robert woke up and noticed his phone was flashing, indicating he had one message. It was from the police department. The police was letting him know his store alarm went off and he need to go there as soon as possible to check it out. He sprung up out of bed, like a firefighter going to a fire call. He took a quick shower and brought his phone into the bathroom, frantically thinking he didn't want to miss another call. He turned the bathroom light on, but it flickered and went out. He did a quick shave and dried himself off and ran back into the bedroom. He got dressed quickly and slightly woke Sarah and told her he had to go to the shop, the police left a message that the store alarm went off, and also mentioned to her that the bathroom light was out and he would change it later.

Still half asleep, she nodded her head and said softly, "OK, baby."

He kissed her on the forehead good-bye and quickly left.

Meanwhile, the morning went on. Sarah felt as though she had been sleeping long and realized her alarm did not go off. She had to move quickly to get the girls off to school on time. She woke them up, fed them, and got them off to school fast. She dropped them off, told them she loved them. They left the car and hustled up the school stairs so they wouldn't be late. Sarah got back to the house. She opened the door, ran to the bathroom, and removed her jogging suit, which she had put on to drop the girls off at school. She didn't bother to turn the bathroom light on, already knowing the bulb was blown, by the conversation she had earlier with Robert. She proceeded to put cream on her face and turned on the shower. She took a nice, hot steamy shower. She loved the hotness of the water. It relax her and at the same time massaged her mind, as well as stimulated her when each drop of water fell on her breasts and ran down her nipples or directly hit them.

As she got lost for a few seconds with the touch of the water, she quickly turn off the shower. Still feeling the tingling of the water on her skin. She stepped out of the tub to dry herself off and then put on her cotton but pretty shower robe. With her robe untied, she started putting on her eyeliner, while her hair was tied up in a towel. Every now and then, she admired herself and her body. Even though Robert lacks telling her, she knows he adores her and her body structure. She is a confident woman, and deep down, she feels her husband appreciates her.

Meanwhile she totally forgot that she was not the only one home. Jazz was now waking up to go to work. He usually walked to work. He knew he could get to work in no time. He walked fast and sometimes slightly jogged. He knew his job was physical, and he was in good physical shape.

One may think he is a professional athlete by his structure and build; and at the height of six feet two, him not being an athlete will be surprising to others. So he jumped out of bed, stretching widely and looking at the clock in his room, knowing he had to get going to be on time. With a T-shirt and boxers on, he was comfortable walking to the bathroom, because normally, he was the only one home in his mind.

He felt this was his own domain. This was the only time the house was empty except for him. As he walked down the hallway, his eyes looking at the wall paintings and mirror-shine shalack floors. He approached the bathroom door. It was slightly closed, and the light switch was off. He never got the word or memo that the light switch in the bathroom didn't work. But as usual, he nonchalantly flicked the switch on to proceed to walk into the bathroom, still not conscious of any shadow about to appear. Sarah too did not hear any steps or movement, so focused on enhancing her beauty. When the door swung open, the breeze from the door struck her like a person on a ship standing on the tip of a boat.

PART 6

Startling her as her eyes grew big as though a freight train getting ready to run her over. As Jazz swung the door open, his eyes realize a figure is in his path as her beauty stood out in his brain. He was still trying to process that someone was here and now in front of him, and in his own mind, in his home.

Now Sarah realize it was Jazz. She was very much startled and slightly observing his sleek, athletic body. He was now faced with the reality that there was someone home, and he felt embarrassed and startled, as though he got caught in the act of robbing a bank. They both looked humbly ashamed. He back up a little away from the door. Her robe was wide open. Her body looked so perfect in his eyes and mind as he stared into her beautiful face. He apologized over and over: sorry, sorry. She did as well, trying to get by the door to leave, as though she had invaded his space and time. She was trying to go out the door as well. But somehow they both could not fit through the door fast enough. Their bodies touched, and they stopped.

Sarah slowly looked up at him.

Jazz looked down at her. Sarah's lips came so close to his chin. Instantly, their lips became coupled. They started kissing each other, the passion of excited sprinted to their hormones. Jazz's penis became rock hard even though they didn't reach the point of intercourse yet. But her hair smelling of a sweet feminine fragrance immediately got his body excited. His hand touched her face as she put her hand over his hand, feeling the strength but soft touch. His hands opened her robe, and her touch for him was getting her body hot. Jazz picked her up, slightly placing her on the edge of the marble sink, lining his penis up to her vagina. He started to try to insert his penis in her vagina with his hands, with his hand brushing against her soaking-wet vagina anxiously wanting him inside her.

Before he was able to put it in, she immediately touched his hand to move it out of the way. She wanted to feel his penis to see what she was up against. The diameter of his penis was breathtaking to her. As she moved her hand down the shaft of his penis, she realized that he was a lot larger than Robert. Jazz, in his mind, was so aroused from her hand moving up and down his penis. Sarah started to put it inside her as Jazz thrust forward to help her to enter it in her body. Feeling so warm and wet, he moved back and forth, slightly pushing the lower part of her body right to the very edge of the sink so her vagina was nearly hanging off the sink edge. His penis was all the way inside, with his testicles bouncing off her bottom cheeks. They both were enjoying each other so much.

Jazz hadn't had sex like this in eight years due to his incarceration. He was losing control and was anxiously getting ready to release his sperm deep in her vagina. Sarah was getting ready to meet him with her orgasm; she felt that he was getting ready to bust, and she wanted this orgasm to be in perfect timing when he started to cum. Like a band with a full orchestra, they both released perfectly and slowed down like a plane just landed on a landing strip. Quickly, they both thought about their jobs.

After fifteen minutes of this escapade, Sarah took a washcloth to quickly wash her vagina as Jazz quickly jumped in the shower. They both got dressed and went to work.

PART 7

Jazz approached his job, for the first time, he entered his workplace with guilt, as though he was entering a courthouse. Still, he walked inside with confidence. He noticed Robert as he entered. Robert said, "Good morning" and smiled.

Jazz smiled and said, "Good morning."

Jazz proceeded to find unopen boxes for the shelves that needed to be restocked. He started to do his job. Although his mind reminisced on the episode this morning. He worked harder to take his mind off of it. Robert called his name abruptly, only to alert him that he had left his phone home and that he needed to run to the house to get it. Robert told Jazz he would be back in fifteen minutes. Jazz said, "OK."

Robert flew home, quickly went into the bathroom, grabbed his phone, and returned to work. Jazz's day moved quickly. Evening came fast. Robert and Jazz closed the store. They both drove home together. Robert put his key in the door.

Mikaela and Caitlin were already coming down the stairs. They yelled their father name when they heard the door open. They hugged him.

Robert asked the girls, "Where's Mommy?"

Mikaela said, "In the bedroom."

Jazz stayed outside for a few minutes and sat on the steps, wondering if he should tell Robert, but mainly just daydreaming.

Sarah came out from the bedroom. She came downstairs and proceeded to the kitchen with Robert, Mikaela, and Caitlin following close behind.

As she was walking to the kitchen, she was telling them all what she had made for dinner. She nonchalantly asked Robert, "Where's Jazz?"

Robert said, "He is outside in the front, just sitting on the steps." Robert came up behind Sarah and kissed her on the neck, indicating their evening might be sexual. Her eyes tried to find his to give him a smile and a flirty smirk. Like, *Yes, can't wait.* Each moment was hard staring at and talking to her husband. She was thinking to herself that she had to build a wall of conscience and not think about what had happened this morning, which she daydreamed of more than usual now.

Robert headed downstairs to his office. His office was nice and clean and neat, more like a man cave with his sports memorabilia, which had professional players' signatures, as well as his own awards when he played from high school, music, and college sports too. His mind would often reminisce to find relaxation. But now he pulled out orders and books that had the store's logs when he needed to order, as well as his phone with notes in there that he had taken for stuff that he would remind himself to order. He had to hustle up a few flights of stairs to go in his bedroom to grab his phone and then went back down to his office. He placed his phone on the big cherrywood desk. He pulled out more papers and receipts to see how much he needed. He grabbed his phone. His phone was like a computer, but he often forgot it. But sometimes he frantically looked for it, like this morning. Now he was going through the steps to retrieve his notes that he had put in the phone throughout the month.

He noticed his phone had been on Record for hours. He took it off Record. He played it back. He thought he might hear people in the store, just to see how things would sound. But instead, he heard moaning and groaning as his eye shift to try to understand like a detective trying to figure out a case. He started to realize the tones he was hearing were tones of his wife. These sounds to him now were like a cannon going off close to his eardrums. These sounds were of intimacy that he heard coming from his own wife. So many feelings were going through him, like a mixtape made by a DJ Anger: sad, mad, just to name a few. His business work came to a halt, as though someone had pulled on the emergency brakes on an Amtrak train.

He eventually went upstairs; he really had no idea what to say or how to approach his wife. He went to their bedroom. She was standing over their bed, reading a business letter or a memo to herself. He tried to have a businesslike look on his face and said to her, "I need you to come downstairs to talk to you pertaining to the house."

She seemed calm but concerned. She started to walk first, asking Robert, "What is it?"

Now they entered the room. His phone, in his eyes, looked like the book of evidence, the Bible. Something that spoke the truth. Robert told her, "Have a seat." He sat behind his desk as though he was talking to a client. He picked up his phone and pressed Play and laid it down.

She listened with no intention that something happened to her. What she was about to hear would shatter her soul and mind. When the phone started playing. She tuned her ears like a German shepherd listening to a command. The moans and groans started, each one more intense than the last. Robert was staring at her as though he was reading her movement to indicate guilt. She was frantically looking for words to come out of her mouth for a defense. She was remembering each moan and every position in every individual moan.

She suddenly said, "Oh my God! I can't believe this!" Her expression and words did not indicate this wasn't her.

PART 8

She immediately said, "You are watching me!. Taping me! In our own house!"

That phrase and answer got to him.

Robert immediately screamed, "Bullshit! That's all you have to say?" Robert went on to say, "How could you? What made you want to do this to me? What made you want to do this to me? To us? And to our family?"

Sarah said, "You didn't trust me."

"I can't believe this," Robert said. "I did trust you! Until now!"

Sarah said, "Then why did you record me?"

Robert said, "I didn't." He went on to say, "I left my phone in the bathroom when I frantically got a phone call from the police saying that the store was burglarized. I jumped out of the bed and got into the shower and forgot my phone."

Sarah recalled him being excited about the police. As she stared in memory, she also remembered Jazz putting her on the sink when they were having sex. In the height of all that, her hand or Jazz must have hit Record on Robert's phone.

Robert continued, "During the day, I realized I didn't have my phone. And I remembered I left it at the house. So I went home during work and grabbed it, put it in my pocket, never thought about it. Till this evening, when I had to retrieve information I put in the phone for the store's inventory. And that's when I discovered your unfaithfulness."

Sarah started crying. She said, "I'm sorry. I love you, and this is not an affair. And I want to fix this."

Robert said, "How could you say this? You was caught in the act moaning like a wounded animal. You're only sorry because you got caught. You bitch! How could you do this? I love you."

Sarah screamed, "Stop it!" She ran upstairs, ran into her bedroom, and slammed the bedroom door.

Robert heard it from downstairs. That evening, they slept in different rooms. Robert slept on the couch in his office. He was comfortable; the couch was huge. He was just so mad he didn't want to have anything to do with her or see her. It was getting late. Sarah was waiting and hoping Robert would come upstairs soon. She had in her mind that she was going to make passionate love to him to convince him she was still madly in love with him and he was the only man in her life. But Robert never showed up. He slept downstairs.

Jazz was in his room. He heard them arguing a little but couldn't make it out. It wasn't clear as it usually was when they argued. Maybe because they were not in the bedroom—they were in Robert's office. But vaguely hearing words like "You bitch! How could you!" from Robert had Jazz's heart beating fast; he was worried that Robert might have found out that he had sex with his wife. Then Jazz thought he might be letting his guilt or imagination run away with him. Little did he know he was right on point.

So as the evening blend into nighttime, the house was quiet. You could hear a pin drop. The wind that night started to pick up sounded like a scene in a horror movie. Sarah got up in the middle of the night. She couldn't sleep. Robert and Sarah were never apart in bed; they made a vow to always sleep together regardless of any argument. But I guess neither one of them could have thought of this happening. She went to the kitchen to get a glass of water. Just standing there, drinking the cold water. They bought Fiji water, poured it into a pitcher, and kept it in the refrigerator. She was now remembering the argument, the phone, Robert's face as he was screaming at her. She was suddenly feeling anxiety, and that Robert was going to leave her. She was looking around the kitchen as though it was her first time being there. Stainless steel appliances and silverware hanging. All of a sudden, the knife selection became the center of affection in her mind. They were hanging on the wall as well.

Like trophies in a hallway. She grabbed a knife, slowly looking at the handle and the point. Noticing the words "stainless steel" on it. She slowly started walking to the basement door where Robert's office was. Her robe was open, her stride of her walk have her robe swinging with her silk nightwear on, and her breast nipples appeared to be hard. She gripped the basement door handle and gently opened it.

Slowly she went down the stairs, although it felt like an eternity to reach the bottom of the staircase. Hearing her heartbeat in her ear like a symphony drum. She made a slight left as she walked a little farther, and there Robert lay. He was sound asleep on his stomach, looking like a crime scene victim that been outlined in a murder scene. Robert was sleeping so peaceful. Sarah continued to take smaller steps toward him. She was standing nervously over him. She raised the knife in her hand and leaped onto his back. She started stabbing him, as if she heard a gun go off to start a road race.

Stabbing him from his head, neck, back, and shoulders. She was stabbing as if she had seen words saying, "stab here, stab here." She was straddling his back, pushing his head into the pillow. Blood was pouring from his body as though it was an open gel cap. As he slept with a free mind. The first knife plunge felt like a toothache pain lifting a nerve from a tooth when you drank something cold with an unfilled cavity. The pain crept up on him, feeling as though he was in a bad dream and wanting to wake up. The stabbing kept happening to his body spontaneously. Never could prepare for the next knife plunge. Finally, he tried to lift his head to turn over, knowing he had to turn over, but he was getting weaker by the second; but now, trying to throw her off him, he manage to do just so. But it wasn't good enough; her adrenaline allow her to leap back onto him. He was now on his back. She was once again straddling his body. What he thought was a dream or a nightmare was reality. The reality of his assailant being his wife. She never lost her rhythm in the stabbing position—stabbing his neck, face, and hands as he tried to defend himself and to grab her hands. Shock and sadness were running through his mind. But he knew he needed to stay focused on stopping her and ultimately to survive.

Unfortunately, his breathing was so spiratic as she continued to plunge the knife all over his body in front, finally hitting his heart.

He felt the pain like none of the others, and it brought his defense to an ultimate stop. He was losing consciousness, but she continue to stab him in his lower stomach and legs. She finally stabbed him a few more times before coming to a stop after seeing no movement from him.

Sarah was breathing heavily as though she had run a marathon. The whole episode lasted only a little over seven minutes. His body was finally silent. His mind was showing and reflecting on his past life experience. Like his marriage to Sarah and the birth of his two little girls by the woman who had his children but passed away having their second child when the first one was only three years old. When she was delivering the second one, she was having an asthma attack while delivering and pass away. These flashes passed through his own mind as his life was slipping away with each second.

PART 9

Although his wife was now a murderer and realizing she had been downstairs for a while. She thought the kids and Jazz were going to wake up, but in reality, she had been down stairs for only twelve minutes. So she rolled him up in the bloody quilt that was on the sofa bed and dropped his body from off the sofa bed to the floor. Then she folded the sofa bed back to the sofa position and placed his body behind the sofa. The kids sometimes looked for their dad and spontaneously come downstairs to say good-bye to him. She was trying to foresee all these things to buy herself time. She went to the bathroom to take a quick shower. She was trembling when she turned on the shower knob on. She scrubbed herself aggressively. She started to cry, wishing she could change things.

From the sex with Jazz to the murder of Robert. She came out of the shower and lay down, trying to take what happened off her mind. Surely, that did not happen.

But what did happen was the alarm clock went off like always. She was happy because she could get the kids off to school and not just think about what she just did. She went to the girls' room. Mikaela was still sleeping. She stared at her for a moment, admiring how much she looked like Robert. Sarah said to Mikaela, "My beautiful princess, wake up. It's time to get dressed for school."

Mikaela turned over and stretched her arms and said, "OK."

Sarah went to Caitlin's bed and said the same thing.

Caitlin responded, "OK, Mommy." Their clothes were already laid out, and the girls went to the bathroom. Sarah went down stairs and made their breakfast. They ate quickly, and then Sarah drove them to school. Sarah dropped them off, looked them both in the eyes and told them she loved them. The girls got out of the car and said almost in harmony, "I love you too, Mommy."

Sarah sped back to the house. She got to the house, made herself some coffee before proceeding to get herself ready for work. She heard Jazz coming down the hallway, and she now realized the store was not open and Robert would have been at the store by now.

Jazz heard her at the kitchen table. Jazz said, "Good morning."

Sarah said, "Good morning." She immediately said to Jazz, "Robert is not here. He had to take care of some important business."

Jazz continued to stare at her. She continued, "You have to open and close the store until he returns."

Jazz was taken aback by her words. Sarah had her head down as she was explaining to him; but she realized he was not saying anything, so she looked up. She said in a demanding voice, "You need to go now!" Jazz finally responded, "When will he be back?"

Sarah said, "I don't know yet." She gave him the keys.

Jazz washed up and quickly headed out the door, like a firefighter heading to a fire.

Sarah felt that went smoothly, no questions. She grabbed yesterday's newspaper. The weather icon caught her eye. She also saw that the tide would be high in a few days.

Although she seemed to be calm, the body of her husband lay dormant downstairs, and if it stayed there longer, it would start stinking and decomposing, and ultimately rigor mortis would set in and the scent would immediately fill the house. Sarah got dress and left for work. Things went on as normal with Sarah. She pick The girls up from School on the way home she mention to the girls that their dad is on a business trip and he will be back home soon. She fixed the kids dinner like always. But instead of waiting for Jazz, she left him a note saying the food was in the oven, and if he was not hungry, could he please put the food in the refrigerator. Sarah was trying to stay out of Jazz's way and avoid questions.

She also mentioned to Jazz in the note that she was not feeling well and did not want to be disturbed. The next morning, things went a little better Sarah got up focusing on the girls and getting them off to school, which went well. When she got back home, Jazz was gone. Sarah went down stairs she started to stare at the office, making sure things looked normal, adjusting the sofa.

She was on the road of denial and deceit. Once the office area was to her satisfaction, she went upstairs to get dressed and to head to work. As days past.

PART 10

One day after picking the girls up from school. Sarah had been embedding herself into her children more than ever. They all arrived home. One of the girls, Mikaela, had a keen nose, and upon entering the house, she said to her sister Caitlin, "You passed gas," and started laughing. Robert's body was starting to smell through the house.

Caitlin responded, "No! I didn't."

Caitlin was now getting angry and was telling Mikaela, "Stop saying bad things to me!"

In the meantime, Sarah was shocked by what came out of Mikaela's mouth.

Sarah interrupted the two and yelled, "Stop!" And then added, "What should we eat for dinner?" Sarah was trying to process both conversations. But she did reluctantly smell the odor fuming from the house.

After eating with the girls, Sarah noticed Jazz was not home. She called the store. Jazz answered. She said, "Hi, it's Sarah. Just making sure things are OK,"

Jazz said, "Hi. Just locking up, and I should be home shortly."

Sarah said, "OK," and hung up the phone.

As the girls were now in their room after dinner, playing or on the computer, Sarah quickly unlocked the downstairs door, saturated the office area with bleach and disinfected. It was so quick and sloppy she threw it down on the floor like she was putting out a fire and wanted the flames to disappear. Then she ran back upstairs. She heard the doorbell and went to the door.

It was Jazz. He said, "Hi."

She said, "Hi." She asked, "How was your day?"

Jazz smiled and said, "Great!"

When Sarah walked in front of him he was checking out her sexy walk and was admiring her and thinking how lucky Robert was. Jazz noticed Sarah had cleaning gloves on. He said, "Cleaning?"

Sarah said, "Yeah. Nothing big. Just some things I wanted to get to before the weekend."

Jazz said, "Oh."

Sarah said, "I'll fix you a plate and leave it on the table. We ate already."

Jazz said, "OK." He went upstairs to clean up a little from work.

As Jazz was eating, Sarah came down to talk to him for a while. Jazz said, "How is Robert doing?"

Sarah said sadly, "He is OK."

Jazz said, "What's wrong?"

As if he detected, Sarah said, "I miss him."

Jazz felt sympathy for her. He said, "He should be home soon."

Sarah just shook her head in agreement with him and said, "Yeah."

Sarah then said, "I need to give you the house key. Just in case the girls and I are not home one day."

Jazz said, "OK." Jazz was so happy things were going well. He was finished eating.

Sarah said, "I'll do the dishes."

Jazz said, "OK." Then he got up from the table and went to his room. They both went their separate ways. As she was doing the dishes, she stared out the window, and she could see her backyard. She brilliantly realized her home had a manhole in the yard. It was called a tide gate. Because the tide would ultimately get high sometimes, but eventually, the water flowed back out to sea. Having this in their yard when Robert purchased, the house, he was able to get the house cheaper. No one liked a manhole on their property. She hadn't come up with how to get Robert's body to there, but she was definitely going to use that to get the body out of the house. And eventually off the property.

She finished the dishes and went to her bedroom. Disposing of Robert's body was still on her mind, wondering whether to wait till two or three in the morning to drag him into the backyard. The houses were far apart, and she was thinking no one was likely to see her. But she was also thinking if the kids woke up and saw her, that would break her heart. So as she lay in bed. She was also thinking that on Friday after school, she would bring the girls over to her family house to visit for the weekend.

Sarah was feeling confident and thinking that everything was sounding great. Although Jazz would more than likely be there, Sarah knew he slept like a log. She remembered that when she was up the night of the murder, she heard him snoring down the end of the hallway before she jumped into the shower.

PART 11

So she made preparations for her family to take the girls on Friday. So that Saturday, she did her house cleaning and paid some bills. Usually, Robert paid them. Sarah missed him but she fought the sadness. She was excited and anxious to move Robert's body. The house was saturated with ammonia and house-cleaning products.

Meanwhile, Jazz was waking up going to get dressed to open the store. He was really comfortable with this. But that Saturday morning, as he was waking up, there was an odor in his room. The room was warm, so the smell was very intense. He wondered, did an animal died in between the walls?

But now he realized the smell was coming from the house vents like the duct work from central heating. He found the spot in his room that the scent was coming from, although he did not know where it led.

But as the scent got so intense, his mood and memory did as well. He was remembering the body in his crime. Although he didn't do the murder. The guy he helped moved the body still made him an accomplice. Which got him prison time: seven years' incarceration. He was still a little angry from the whole ordeal. Still saying to himself, *This can't be true. In the house? Of this family? A body?*

Jazz remembered Sarah's face as she told him about the store. He was swmurking. But he was very suspicious about her story of Robert. He got up from the squatting position and stood up and proceeded to leave his

---

bedroom. As he left his bedroom slowly walking down the hall. Examining the hall like he was a detective looking for clues and something to convince him that Sarah had been lying to him. He was just getting ready to go in the bathroom because he also needed to prepare to go to work. Suddenly, he heard movement in the kitchen. He continued to stroll down the hall to the kitchen. He found Sarah at the kitchen table rambling through bills and processing statements.

She glanced up and noticed him standing there. He had a towel in his hand as if he was going to the bathroom. Sarah said, "Hi."

Jazz said, "Good morning." He quickly asked, "Where are the girls?"

She said. "They are over at my family's house." She also said, "I took them last night." She dropped her head and then quickly raised it and said, "Why?"

Jazz said, "I *would* like to talk to you."

She said, "Are you going to work?"

"It won't take long," he said. "Did you ever have a problem with squirrels or raccoons in the house?"

Sarah said, "No . . . why?"

He said because he smelled something, and it appeared to be dead.

She quickly got annoyed, even showing guilt. She replied sarcastically, "Oh, really. You're an expert on dead smells."

He smirked and said, "Well, no, but I have smelled a few dead things in my life."

She found his answer and his smile to be annoying. She quickly addressed him as a boss would his employee and said, "You should really be getting ready to go to work."

He asked her, "When is my boss coming back?"

She quickly answered him with an attitude: "Why?"

He looked at her like that was a dumb answer. He replied, "I need him to order some things, and I need to talk to him about the cash flow."

"He didn't show you?"

He said, "No."

She said, "Leave me the supply order, and I will take care of it. And I will also stop by to collect the cash flow." Sarah was speaking to him in a somewhat cocky and disrespectful manner.

Jazz got up from the table and walked a few steps, like he was heading to the bathroom. He turned around to look at her. She had returned to writing out some things she had to take care of. Jazz felt the way she looked had guilt written all over her face. He just stopped in his tracks and said, "You still didn't answer my question."

She replied, "About what?"

He said, "Where is my boss? And when will he return?"

Sarah said, "Look! I do not owe you any explanation about my husband."

Jazz blurted out, "If something's wrong, I can help."

Sarah threw her pen down that was in her hand. She got and walked toward the kitchen window and looked out. She replied, "I'm fine," in a soft, sad voice. She said, "You need to go to work. It's getting late."

He took a chance on his hunch and said, "If it was an accident, I can help you."

She turned around from the window and looked at him, as if to say, *What the fuck are you talking about.* But she never said these words. But her face had that expression. She was looking guilty. His statement of pleading to help was wearing her down.

Jazz walked toward her at the kitchen window. She was staring in his eyes. He was staring back into hers, as if he was saying, *You can trust me. Please let me help you.*

In a desperate look, she was staring at him. As if she was about to confess to a priest. With a humble *I fucked up* type of look. They were just staring at each other. Not a word. Not a murmur. He was trying to will her: *Please give me something.*

Slowly, water of tears came from her eyes. She stepped to the side and walked by him. She blurted out, "He knows."

Jazz felt as though he had broken through and she was letting him in. But he was confused. He replied, "He knows what?"

She was standing at the kitchen table with both hands violently gripping the back of the chair. She replied, "He knows you fucked me!"

Jazz was still standing there with a *What the fuck!* look on his face. He responded, "But how?"

Sarah slowly paused, as though she was running a marathon. She went on to say, "He got up early because the police called and said the store alarm was sounding. He got out of bed and frantically took a shower, got dressed, and left. But he left his phone in the bathroom. When you was fucking me, you or I must have hit Record on his phone."

Jazz was staring at her, watching her lips make every word. Like he was lip reading. Jazz said, "Don't blame yourself. He could have hit Record when he was in the bathroom."

She said. "No! It was us!"

There was silence. He felt as though he had done a crime and was going back to jail. She immediately started crying. He touched her arm and then said, "So he left you?" She looked at him like she didn't want to tell him. Jazz said, "Sarah! Where is he?"

So she said softly, "I killed him."

Jazz said, "What! What! What are you talking about?"

He said, "How?" He shook her by the shoulders and said, "Sarah!"

She glared up at him and said, "I killed him. I thought he was going to leave me. I did wrong. He would have taken everything."

Jazz said, "How did you do it?" He was grabbing her by the shoulders.

She started crying. She said, "I kept stabbing him over and over until he didn't move."

He let go of her shoulders, stepped back, and his eyes were saying, "Oh my God." But he stayed focused. He didn't want to spook her.

Sarah said, "I'm going to the police."

Jazz said, "No!" She stared at him, and he said, "You will go to jail. What about the girls? We can get through this. Where's the body?" Then Jazz said, "Wait! is that what I smell?" He said this a few times.

Sarah finally said, "Yes."

Jazz said, "We gotta get rid of the body."

She look up at him and said, "We?"

He said, "Yes. I will help you."

She looked at him. Her eyes were saying, *Thank you so much.*

They hugged, and Jazz said, "Where's the body?"

She said, "Downstairs in his office."

He told her he needed to go down there. She slowly went to the table and picked up her keys. She opened the door to downstairs. Jazz hesitated. He looked back at her and proceeded to walk down the stairs slowly. He looked at everything. This was his first time down there. Sarah was behind him. He was walking like he was in a scary house. He really didn't see the body. But the smell was everywhere. He covered his nose. He turned around and look at her and said, "Where is the body?" As if he didn't have a clue.

She said, "Behind the sofa."

He spotted the sofa and slowly walked toward it. And there he lay, wrapped in a quilt and a sheet. She started crying, so they both turned around and went back upstairs. Jazz paused after he closed the door and locked it. He said, "We got to get him out of here before the kids come back."

Sarah said, "They won't be back till Sunday night."

He looked at her and said, "Is that why you sent them to the family?"

She said, "Yes."

Jazz said, "I take it you got a plan."

She started crying again.

He said, "What?" As if she had another surprise of bad news for him. But she didn't. She said in between tears and crying that she was going to drag him out of the house. "But I can't lift him." She said that with no pressure of the kids being around, she could drag him to the backyard.

He said, "Backyard? Why there?"

Sarah said, "There is a manhole cover behind the house." She continued, "We got the house at a cheap price because of the high tide that sometimes flooded the ground. The tide eventually goes down, and the water goes back out to sea."

Jazz said, "Oh, I understand. So if you can get the body there, then it will go out to sea."

She quietly said, "Yes." She started to weep some more.

He pulled her into his arms slowly and said, "It's going to be fine. I'm going to help you. Don't worry. We're in this together."

She looked up at him as if to say, *Thank you.* He told her he had to get to the store now. He said, "We have to do things normal, so it won't raise no attention." She silenced silently shake her head yes to confirm. Jazz said, "We will move his body tonight when it's dark."

They hugged in a tight partner way to reassure each other. He raised her face and said, "It will be OK." They slowly kissed, longer than they should have. With her beauty and touch, immediately his penis started getting hard. She felt it while kissing him, and she massaged his dick with her hand. She found the opening to his boxer shorts and pulled his penis out, and her lips left his face, and she slowly lowered her face as if her face was an elevator pressed to go down to his penis. And she gave him a blowjob before he got dressed for work. He was totally enjoying the five-minute blowjob. With her lips covering the head of his penis, soaking the head of his cock, he put his penis down her throat and rapidly did it over and over again. He finally ejaculated, and she swallowed it. This was a message thanking him for understanding and for helping her dispose of the body. In his mind, he felt this was a relationship. He felt totally committed to her and wanted to demonstrate the same to reassure her. The sexual event came to an end within five minutes. They both realized they were late for their jobs. And although it was Saturday and they had a later start time than during the week, they were still under pressure to get to work.

As the day went on, Jazz was working and thinking about that evening. He was anxious all day to get back to the house and was contemplating the best time to remove Sarah's husband's body. It was a struggle for him to stay focused on his store duties, but he knew he had to. Everything relied on him. In a lot of ways, he felt that the store was his since he knew now that Robert was not coming back. He never had opportunities in his life coming from a family of nine, him being the second from the oldest. He either had hand-me-downs or he never accomplished things to his liking. But now he had confidence in this whole situation. Even in this plot, he felt this it's his way he had to make this a success.

So as the day became evening, he did what he usually did—close out the cash, took inventory. Once his routine was done, he closed the store and hurried home. As he approached the house, he felt different. His thought process on entering the house was more relaxed. He really was content, and the best part was, he was coming home to Sarah. He got to the house and opened the door. The house smelled clean, but she had been cleaning everything. She changed the house around as well.

He said, "Hi."

She said, "Hi. And just continue moving stuff around."

Jazz shrugged his shoulders and continued to his room. He opened the door and stopped to smell the room. The smell was still there, if not worse. He changed his clothes, took a shower, and then he went downstairs. She asked Sarah, did she cook?

She replied, "Why? My children are not here."

He stared at her; she stared at him, smiled, and said, "Yes, it's in the microwave."

He smiled back. He ate and then went to the living room and turned the TV on. She looked at him weird as he was watching the TV show that was on. Then he felt her eyes on him; it was her, still staring. He felt weird, but he knew she was looking at him because he was in the living room. He started explaining to her slowly. He said, his room? She was waiting for him to finish. He continued, "It smells in there." She just walked away and finished cleaning. She was finishing the girls' room.

Once she finished the girls' room, she took a shower and drank some wine. She looked at the clock, then looked outside from a window in her room. She noticed it was getting dark. She was looking at some papers from work, and before she knew it, she was asleep. Mostly tired from stressing over the crime. She was feeling a little relieved that Jazz would help take care of it. He was stretched out on the couch. He fell asleep right there while watching a television show. The sofa was big and had plenty of space for him to stretch out. It was dark outside, and the house was quiet. All you could hear was the TV and his slight snoring. A loud commercial came on the TV, and he nearly stood straight up. Then he realized it was the television. He looked around the clean house just to grab his thoughts. He was still listening to her snore, but there was total silence you he started he was heading to her bedroom.

He looked into the girls' room. The room was spotless. Then he looked into her bedroom next. There she was. In his mind, she looked so sexy. He got closer to her, slightly shook her to wake her up. He leaned over her. She turned over, and all she could see was his face and his brown eyes; his eyes looked light against his skin. Once he felt she was aware of her surroundings, he then told her it was time. She shook her head to confirm. He slowly grabbed her little hand and led her to the downstairs door. Showing her ownership and control of the situation. Then went downstairs slowly; he was leading her, still looking around as though he was sneaking around to do something.

Jazz said to Sarah, "How do you open the manhole cover?"

She said, "There is a certain tool he has in the garage." She walked to the garage through the downstairs office door, took a right and a quick left. That was the tool area. She immediately spotted the tool and went back and showed him.

He shook his head to say OK. He walked to the office door that led to the backyard, stepped outside to see if he could spot the manhole cover. He asked Sarah, "Do you have a small flashlight?" She said yes. She looked into Robert's office drawer. She had seen him with one sometimes, and she saw him put it back there. Jazz told her that it was time. Sarah picked up the flashlight and the pick and led him to the manhole. He walked behind a sofa, and really didn't want to do this. But he signed up for this. He thought about the blowjob he got from Sarah, and now he knew it was time to pay the piper. Jazz bent down to grab the body, and he realized how stiff it was. It felt like a flagpole or a manican doll. He picked up the body, keeping all the garments with it. It immediately remind him of his previous crime, and he couldn't believe this was happening again. But now he felt he was experienced and knew not to get caught.

He was marching behind Sarah as she led him to the manhole, not saying a word. She was developing a tough skin, although she was feeling sad, but she was not crying at this moment. She was focused on getting to the manhole. Jazz was starting to realize how heavy Robert's body was. It felt as though he had walked one block, but in essence, it was only thirty to forty feet from the office door. He arrived at the manhole, and Sarah turned and looked at him.

Jazz told her to open it. She took the hook and put it in the manhole. She struggled to pull it off, just like Robert used to struggle. Jazz released him from his arms. The hole was about twenty-five-plus feet deep. As Sarah shone the light down there, Jazz slowly turned and angled the quilt and sheet in a vertical position with Robert still wrapped in it. Jazz's feet was close to the manhole's edge. Jazz opened his arms, dropping the body straight down to the huge hole at the bottom. He took the flashlight from Sarah and noticed part of Robert's body could still be seen. He told her, "Oh no!"

She said, "What?"

He said, "I can still see the body."

She explain how the tide would come, and it would become extremely high and push everything that was in the manhole straight out to the ocean.

He said, "Really?"

She said, "Yes. I will check tomorrow to find out when the next tide comes in to be high. It should be soon." They both start feeling that they should go back to the house. Now he put the cover back on the manhole and noticed it was extremely heavy, and there was no way she could have done any of this by herself.

After the manhole was sealed, they started to walk quickly back to the house, going into the office door again. The walk felt a lot quicker than going to the manhole. She walked into the door first, and he came in second. He immediately turned around to lock the tightly secure door.

He let out a sigh. He actually felt sad, and she did too. He held her and quietly said, "It's over." She just held him, so they released and headed upstairs.

Jazz sat on the couch and just stared at the walls, feeling as though he was back in the criminal world, sadly thinking he was trying to do so right. She broke through his daydream and said she would be in her room. Then she turned and walked away. Sunday came, and he woke up on the couch. He went into his room. The room still smelled a little, so he opened his windows. He took some Febreze air freshener earlier from work, and now he sprayed the room, got under the covers, slightly stressed over the situation. Then he eventually went back to sleep.

Actually, Jazz slept till eleven thirty. He got up and walked to the bathroom and urinated. He had on a t-shirt and a pair of boxes on no one home but him and Sarah. He heard noise in the front toward the kitchen. It was Sarah. She was rearranging things in the kitchen. She stopped and looked up. Jazz said, "It looks nice."

She said, "Thank you." Sarah mentioned she made waffles for him.

Jazz smiled and said, "Yes, thank you." And he sat down and ate. She was watching him. He was thinking she had something to say, so he said, "What's up?"

Sarah said, "Nothing." She added, "Well, I just wanted to thank you."

Jazz paused with his food in his mouth. He said in a firm voice, "You're welcome, and this should never be talked about."

She was kind of taken back by his statement. She said, "Are you OK?"

He said, "Yeah." He added, "Robert was a good, kind man."

She said, "Are you blaming me?"

He said, "Maybe you was overreacting. He loved you."

She was getting sad and mad. She said, "He was going to leave me, and I knew he would have taken everything from me. I wish I could change things, but I can't."

Jazz resumed eating.

Sarah got up. She stepped away and then turned around and said, "Are you OK? Or should I be worried about you?"

Jazz said, "Me? Please. I'm the least of your worries. Remember, I am an accomplice. Anyways, relax. We will be fine." As she was walking away, he said, "When are the girls coming home?"

She said, "This evening," and kept walking, heading to the living room. She had changed the living room around and cleaned it, trying to erase the way things were when Robert was alive and at home. Jazz got through eating, took a quick shower, and headed to the gym. He goes on Sundays. He works out for long hours. Sarah finally finished rearranging the house. She stepped back, and she didn't see a trace of Robert. Meaning she felt better, but sad. Each day was getting better for her, especially since Jazz was her codefendant. She picked up the phone and called her sister Emily, who had the kids. She told Emily she would be there in a couple of hours to get the kids. Sarah also asked how the girls were doing.

Emily said, "OK." She asked Sarah how Robert was, and she said, "He is out of town." Quickly, Sarah said she had to go. "But we'll be there soon."

Emily said, "OK."

Sarah picked up the girls from her sister Emily's house. The girls said they had fun and Aunt Emily took them to the children's museum on Saturday. Sarah replied, "That must have been fun."

The girls asked, "Is Daddy home?" The girls said they missed Daddy so much.

Sarah had tears in her eyes, but she quickly wiped them. When they got home, they noticed their mom had changed the house around and cleaned their room. They both said they liked it. Sarah asked, were they hungry? She made a chicken casserole, their favorite; and they had chocolate pudding for dessert. Then they went to their room: one played on the computer, and the other one watched TV.

Jazz had just come in from the gym. Sarah saw him, and she smiled. She was admiring how good he looked. He had on a tank-top shirt fitting his body type. Since their episode, her body get wet for him. She smirked and said hi, and he smiled and went to his room to take a shower; and she said as he walked to his room, "I made chicken casserole, and the girls are home."

He said, "That's good." He also said he would be there to eat after he took a shower.

"She said, OK."

Later, he came down, made himself a plate, and he started eating. He looked up at her. She had put on some perfume, and he commented on it. "It smells good."

She said, "Thanks."

As he was eating, he touched her hand and said, "Thank you for the food." His hand over hers power her little hand. You could not see her hand on the table once he put his hand over it. They were staring at each other, and just as they were in that position, Mikaela came around the corner to ask her mom a question and noticed Jazz's hand over her mom's hand.

Mikaela stared at his hand and then looked at him, then at her mom.

Jazz dropped his eyes, removed his hand quickly, and finished his food. Sarah stood up to ask Mikaela, "What can I do for my pretty little girl?"

Mikaela replied, "Can I have a glass of milk please?" The girls were always well mannered. Mikaela got angry as she thought about jazz holding her mom's hand. She said loudly, "When will Dad be home?" As if she couldn't wait to tell him.

Jazz kept his head down, but he was feeling every thought of Mikaela.

Sarah said, "I told you soon." Sarah also told Mikaela, "He got a surprise for you and your sister when he comes home."

Jazz looked up at Sarah, and Mikaela said, "Really?" with a big smile. She loved when her dad bought her things. She was definitely Daddy's little girl. Sarah would say anything to take her thoughts off what Mikaela had just seen.

Mikaela took the milk and returned to her room. Jazz got up from the table to put the dishes away. He stared at Sarah.

She said, "What?"

Jazz said, "Why did you tell her that lie? That her father got a surprise for her and her sister?"

Sarah said, "I only tried to take her mind off from what she had seen— you holding my hand."

He shook his head and went to his room. Jazz didn't like what Mikaela had seen. And it made him angry

As nighttime drew near, everybody were in their room. Sarah had changed her bedroom around as well. She appeared to sleep better.

Jazz wanted to hurt Mikaela. He didn't trust her, and he was thinking the worst. But as they all woke up, they were all late for their jobs and school. Sarah took Jazz in the car but dropped off the girls first and drove him and dropped him off at the job. She said "Bye" with a sexy smile. He just said "Bye" with a straight face. Little did they know the nightmare was slowly creeping up on them.

Monday, a jogger was running near the shoreline and discovered what appeared to be the body of a white male. It was breaking news and in all the local papers. Sarah picked up the kids from school as usual. She told the girl she had to stop at the store to get some drinks for dinner. She went in a quick store near the <u>school. As</u> she was paying for her purchases, the store owner had the TV on, and it was breaking news, and they both heard that there was a body discovered near the shoreline. She quickly got the drinks and left the store.

Stopping at the store with the kids near their school to get something to drink for dinner in the store the owner had a television on, and it was a news flash that caught her attention. On the TV, it read a body came up onshore. She immediately had the cashier ring up her drinks and walked fast back to the car.

The kids saw her face was filled with anxiety.

She quickly told the girls to buckle up.

When she entered the house, she told the girls to go upstairs and clean up and their dinner would be on the table. Then she thought about calling Jazz at the shop, but she changed her mind.

Instead, she called the local police.

Officer McDermott answered. He said, "This line is being recorded."

She said, "My name is Mrs. Sarah McKinley, and my husband is missing."

The officer asked her when she last saw her husband. She said, "Last Monday. He went on a business trip, but he usually calls me."

The officer ask her, "So you're saying it's been over twenty-four hours, correct?"

She said, "Yes."

He told her, "Come down and fill out a missing person report, and we will get back in touch with you."

She said, "OK." She hung up the phone and sat with the kids and ate, but she really couldn't. But when the kids finished, she told them to grab their coats. "Mommy has to go somewhere."

They did So she told them they could bring their portable handheld computer games.

Mikaela said, "Really."

Her mother said, "Yes."

Then they got in the car and left. They arrived at the police station, and she said, I'll be back. I just got a question for the officer. I'll be right back And don't tease your sister."

Mikaela said, "OK."

Sarah went inside, and the officer behind the desk said, "Ma'am, can I help you?"

She said, "Yes, my name is Sarah McKinley. I want to make a missing person report."

He said, "Yes, I talked to you on the phone earlier."

She said, "Oh yes."

The officer gave her the form, and she quickly filled it out and when the last time she had seen him. She signed the document and gave it back to the officer.

Officer McDermott explained to her that if they heard anything, they would definitely get in contact with her.

She sadly said, "Thank you," and left. She walked quickly back to the car. Caitlin, the other sister, said, "All set, Mommy."

She quickly looked at her daughter in shock for her to have said that.

She said yes. Sarah was just a little edgy. She told them to buckle up, and they headed home

They arrived home, and she told the girls to finish their homework and then get dressed for bed. They said, "OK."

The front door opened. Sarah walked toward the front. It was Jazz coming in. He said, "hi." She said, "Hi."

He said, I normally don't say this, but is the food ready? I'm starving."

She smiled and said, "Yes, I'll put it out on the table. Go wash up."

He said, "OK."

As he was eating, she was sitting there, and she asked him, how was his day, and how was the shop? He said, We have to restock soon. It's getting low in the storage area."

She said, "OK."

Then a few seconds of quiet, and then he asked her how her day was, and she said, "A few things happened."

He said, "Oh. I'm listening."

She said, "I picked up the girls from school, went into that variety store that's not that far from their school to get drinks for dinner. The owner has a television in the store. It caught my eye because breaking news was flashing at the bottom saying a body had washed ashore."

Jazz stopped eating as though someone had said "Freeze!" He said, "Oh wow."

She said, "Yeah." She added, "They don't have no information."

He slowly started eating again.

Then she said she went to the police station.

He stopped eating as though someone had threw on an emergency brake. He said, "What!"

She said, "Lower your voice. The kids are home, you know."

He said, "Why did you go to the police station?"

She said, "I went to file a missing person report."

He said, "What did they say?"

"They gave me a form, I filled it out, and they said they will contact me if they hear anything."

Jazz said, "I thought we were in this together. It's my neck out here too."

She said, "I thought I did the right thing."

He said, "From now on, I want to know before you do anything—is that clear?" This reminded her of Robert when they used to argue.

Jazz quietly said to her, "I'm not going back to prison." He felt that people got him caught. He didn't make mistakes. He stood up to take his dishes to the sink.

Sarah came up behind him and rubbed his back and took the dishes from him, rubbing his back saying she is sorry, she wouldn't do it again.

He nodded his head as if to say *OK*.

Mikaela appeared out of nowhere. Sarah felt eyes on her and quickly turned around. Mikaela had already seen her rubbing her back.

Sarah shouted, "Mikaela, what is it?"

Mikaela said, "I can't find my pajamas."

Jazz just snatched his body around and sped by Mikaela, never looking at her, and headed to his room with an angry face for Mikaela.

The next day for Sarah was so hectic. Her alarm didn't go off, and the children barely made it on time for school. When she came back from dropping them off, Jazz had already left, she got dressed and left for work as well.

As the day went on you can well aspect went by quickly. On her way home, her cell phone rang. She picked it up and said, "Hello."

"This is Officer Durant. Can I speak to Sarah McKinley."

She said, "This is she."

He went on to say, "I would like for you to come down to the police department."

She pulled over. She answered, "Why?"

He said, "We had a body that washed up ashore. White male in his late forties. I need you to make an identification of the body."

Sarah said, "Are you saying it's my husband?"

"I'm saying I need you to come down here to rule out this is not your husband."

She said "OK" in a hesitant way

She said, "I'm on my way."

He said, "Good."

When she arrived at the station, an officer said, "May I help you?"

She said, "Yes, I would like to speak to Officer Durant."

He said, "Yes. Hi. You are Sarah?"

She said, "Yes."

He said, "Right this way." As they were walking to the morgue, he mentioned that she would only need to see the face because the body was badly decomposed. He was standing next to the corpse.

He asked her, was she ready? She said yes in a soft voice, and he pulled the sheet back. She screamed, and he pulled it back over and grabbed her. He said, "Was that him?"

She said, "I don't know."

He said, "What do you mean?"

She said his face was bad. He paused as if she had to do it again. Then she said he had a tattoo where she said there was—on his right arm near his shoulder.

Of the football team, he liked the New England Patriots. He liked that team. The officers looked himself, and he told her yes, he did, and she cried terribly. Between guilt and her love for him.

The officer walked her back upstairs. She told the officer she had to go pick up her kids, and the officer walked her to her car. He said, "Ma'am, we don't normally let someone drive being so distraught."

She said, I'll be fine. I gotta pick up my girls." She got into the car and said, "If you need anything, don't hesitate to call us."

She said, "Thank you." She picked up the kids from school, not really making eye contact with them.

Mikaela was smart. She would know something was wrong. Sarah quietly asked them how school was as she was driving. When they arrived home, she told them to do their homework. Dinner would be ready in twenty minutes.

They said, "OK, Mommy."

She made beef gravy and rice—Kaitlin's favorite. When they got through eating, they returned to their room to play on their computer before bedtime.

Sarah was cleaning up the kitchen and then put Jazz's plate in the oven. The doorbell rang. Sarah thought Jazz forgot his key, so she just unlocked the door slightly open, and then turned and walked away. Then the bell rang again. A=she immediately turned back around and had a few bad words for Jazz; but instead, it was a slender white guy in a suit, standing there. She said, "Can I help you?"

He said, "My name is Detective Cornell Patterson. I would like to speak to a Sarah McKinley."

She said, "I'm here." Then she asked, "What is this about?"

He said, "May I come in?"

She said yes and told him to have a seat.

He said, "I'm here to talk about your husband, Robert McKinley."

She said, "About what?"

He said, "About his death. When did you last see him?"

She said, "Two weeks ago. He had a business trip."

Detective Patterson was taking notes. He said, "Your husband was found by a jogger near the ocean shoreline. He only had on a T-shirt and boxers. Multiple stab wounds."

She said, "Please, I can't handle this right now. And my daughters are home in their room. I don't want to cry now."

He said, "I understand. I just want you to know the medical examiner ruled this as a homicide, and I have the case."

As they were in the house talking, Jazz was walking home, getting closer to the house. He recognized the car parked behind Sarah. He realized the plates said Police. He turned around and started walking the other way. His mind was frantically going through scenarios on what they could possibly be asking her.

Detective Patterson told Sarah, "If anything comes to mind, here is my card—please give me a call, and I will be in touch." He stood up and walked toward her door. Then he turned to her and said, "Your husband was brutally murdered, and I'll do my best to find the killer."

She shook his hand and said, "Thank you."

Meanwhile, Jazz saw the police cruiser speed by him. He immediately turned around and headed to the house.

Just as soon as Sarah closed the door, it opened again, and it was Jazz. He had a serious look on his face. He said, "I saw the detective's car in the driveway. I hesitated in coming home." He asked, "What did he say?"

She said, "He said Robert was murdered, and he is going to hunt for whoever is responsible for it."

When Mikaela got to school after their mom dropped her and Caitlin off, Mikaela saw her best friend, Tabitha.

Tabitha said, "Hi, Mikaela. How are you doing?"

Mikaela said, "Fine." Tabitha started crying. Mikaela said, "What's wrong?" She felt all the other kids in her class staring at her. Tabitha hugged Mikaela so hard, and Mikaela said, "I don't understand. It's OK. Why are you sad?"

Tabitha said, "I know, Mikaela. It's OK. I'm here for you, and the other kids too."

Mikaela said, "Did I do something wrong?"

Tabitha started crying and said, "Your dad . . ."

Mikaela said, "My dad?"

Tabitha said, "He died. He was murdered."

Mikaela said, "What! No!" She looked at everyone and screamed over and over.

Teachers ran over, and they said, "Mikaela, it's OK."

She said, "I don't believe you."

The teacher said, "Your mom didn't tell you. It was on the news."

Mikaela was screaming, crying. Then she tried to run. The teacher grabbed her, and Mikaela said, "Let go! I need to see my sister."

At the same time, Caitlin was hearing the news the same way. The teacher brought them together and took them to the office, trying to control them, asking them, "Why haven't you been told?"

They said, "My mom said he is on a trip and he is going to bring us a surprise." They were crying hysterically.

People at Sarah's job heard as well and hugged her touch her and saying if she needed anything, she could count on them.

"Thank you," she said sadly.

They all went back to their cubicles.

Meanwhile Sarah's phone had fourteen missed calls and messages. All from her kids' school. She played back her voice mail. The teacher was explaining that her daughters were very upset. Apparently, they found out through their classmates that their father passed away. "Plz come to the school ASAP."

Sarah quickly spoke to her boss and told him that her children were sick at school and she had to leave immediately.

He said, "It's OK. You can leave." He sympathized with her sensitivity in this time of her life.

Sarah grabbed her wallet and race to her vehicle. She got to the girls' school quickly, hustled up the stairs. Normally, she would have to be buzzed into the school.

The school secretary was at the window, hoping Sarah would arrive. All the faculty were so heartbroken for the little girls, but they had to be strong.

The girls saw their mother and ran a few steps to her and were crying terribly.

The principal said to Sarah, "Can I talk to you for a second?" The principal said, "Girls, this won't be long. I need to talk to your mom. Please sit down in the secretary's office, OK."

They said yes.

The principal told Sarah, "The girls said they had no idea their dad died."

"Why did you tell them?" Sarah said. "This was supposes to happen this evening. You have to understand this got to my ears as well."

The principal stared at her.

Then Sarah said, "Well, a few days ago."

The principal, in closing, said, "This evening, I would encourage you to tell them everything. Leave no question untold. And if they need to speak to someone medically and professionally, you should try to make it happen. If the girls need more time off, please give it to them. This is a traumatic situation."

The principal call herself scolding Sarah for not telling the girls before they came to school.

The principal said nothing more, and Sarah replied, "I understand your concern for the girls, and I will explain to them in our home more appropriately, and I'm sorry for any disruption they might have caused due to my tardiness in explaining to them about their father."

Sarah paused and said, "Are we finished?" As if she was the one in school being chastised.

The principal said sadly, "You have my condolences."

Sarah left with the girls from their school. On the way home, the girls asked their mom to stop at the store, and could they have ice cream? Sarah said, "It's early, but we can buy some and eat it later, OK."

They said, "OK."

Caitlin started crying, and soon after, Mikaela did too. Sarah was quiet and sad.

Mikaela said to her mom, "Who hurt my daddy?"

Sarah quietly said, "The police are still looking for them."

Caitlin said, "I hope they find him."

Mikaela said, "Me too."

Sarah and the kids finally reached home. They went to their room. Sarah's cell phone rang. It was Jazz. She said hello.

He said, "It's me, Jazz."

She said, "Hi."

He said, "You're not going to believe this. When I got to work, there had to be at least a hundred flowers here for Robert. The store's been busy."

She said, "Yeah, I believe it. I had to get the girls from school. I'm home with them."

He said. "Oh, I can only imagine." He said he had to go. "Customers are here." He told her to hang in there. He didn't know it, but she had a smile on her face.

She said, "You too."

A customer came in. He needed this clear epoxy and some Liquid Nails. Jazz got it for him.

The customer said, "Did they catch the killer yet?"

Jazz sadly said, "No."

The customer was so sad. He said, "Robert was a good guy. Will give you the shirt right off his back."

He looked in the customer's eyes and said, "You're right."

The customer said, "Tell his wife, the family, in his prayers."

Jazz said, "I will. And thank you."

The man just turned and left.

Soon it was evening, and the store was closing. Jazz was looking around in the store and noticed he had to stock the store. He closed the store and started walking home.

Sarah made spaghetti. She told the girls to come down to eat. They came and sat down at the table. Jazz also was putting the key in the door and walking in.

She yelled, "We're eating."

He said, "I'll eat later."

Caitlin was getting angry, and Sarah said, "What's wrong, Caitlin?"

She said, "I hope who did this to Daddy dies."

Sarah said, "We have to be strong. Daddy would want us to be strong."

After Jazz washed up and cleaned up, he was starting to go to the kitchen. He heard Mikaela ask Sarah, "So Jazz is going to leave?"

Sarah looked at Mikaela and said, "Why you say that?"

Mikaela said, "Well, since Daddy's not here, he don't need to stay here." Mikaela was fearing the worst. Her emotions were everywhere.

Sarah tried not to get excited, but she said, "Well, she thinks Daddy would want him here because he is running the store. He knows the store." Before Mikaela was able to say another word, she heard Jazz's footsteps getting near the kitchen. She slightly looked up and then dropped her gaze again. She didn't want to see him. Only he knew the thoughts that were going through her mind.

He sat at the table and said, "How is everyone doing?" And then he said to the girls, "Um . . . so sorry about your dad." Quietly, he said, "He was a good man, and will help you girls in any way. He would have wanted me to after he talk."

Mikaela looked at Sarah and said,: Mom, can I get up? I'm finished."

Sarah quietly said, "Sure, my oldest princess."

Mikaela put a smile on her face and excused herself.

Seconds later, Caitlin said, "Me too, Mommy. I'm finished."

Sarah said, "Sure, my youngest princess."

Caitlin smiled too and walked away.

Sarah and Jazz remained at the table. Jazz said, "The spaghetti is good." He said he was so hungry at work. He started to say to Sarah, "You know Mikaela don't like me."

She said, "What makes you think that?"

He said, "I see her drop her eyes and leave every time I come around. I think ever since she saw you touching me, or your hand was on my back."

She said, "I think you're letting your imagination think negative things. She is just everywhere right now because of Robert. She will be OK. It will just take some time." She took his dishes, and she said, "I got ice cream. The girls wanted it but didn't want it after dinner."

He said, "No, I'm OK, thank you." Then he added, "You have to come to the store and make a deposit. It's full, and I have to reorder quickly."

She said, "Maybe Friday."

He said, "OK," and walked to his room.

The next day, the girls and Sarah stayed home. Jazz got up and noticed he didn't hear any movement in the house. He went to the bathroom, got in the shower, got dressed, and left after he stuck a note on Sarah's bedroom door. It read,

I see you guys stayed home. Hope you guys have a nice day. Don't forget I need you to remove the money. I will have a list for you to restock the store.

Jazz left and went to the store. Sarah got up and went to check on the girls in their room and told them, "You guys are staying home today, OK."

They said, "OK." The girls still seemed sad. Sarah called their pediatrician. She was able to talk to her and told her the girls just lost their dad and having a hard time.

The doctor said, "I can talk to them about 11:30 a.m. if you're available."

Sarah said, "Sure. The girls and I are staying home today."

Meanwhile, Detective Patterson got the tide schedule and was able to match everything from the area where Robert McKinley lived, so he was thinking that since he wasn't able to find his car and clothes, he was coming to realize he never left his neighborhood, and it looked like he was killed in his area. He also saw that when high tide came in, it sometimes caused property damage.

He went to the town hall and got prints of the whole area where Robert lived. He realized two homes in that area had tide gates and drain lines on their property. Sarah's place was one of them. Sarah's place had the tide gates that water could flow on to their property and return out to the sea.

He really hated to, but he could not just walk onto her property. He also felt that if she gave him a hard time, she was looking more and more as a suspect. He felt she had already lied to him by saying he took a plane.

He started to call her.

The phone rang, and it immediately went to voice mail. He left her a message asking her to call him back. Detective Patterson was feeling more and more confident that Robert was murdered near his home, if not in his home. But the motive and the reason and the evidence had not been established yet.

Sarah told the girls to get dressed. "We have to go out." She never told them it was to the doctor's office. They would be asking her too many questions Sarah could not <u>answer. As</u> Sarah herself was getting dressed, she saw her cell phone flashing one message. She played it <u>back. It</u> was the detective asking her to call him back. She didn't. Having the kids today and going through their stress would only stress her out; but she was wondering, *What does he want to talk about?* The curiosity was getting to her. She dialed his number back. The phone rang, and he picked up.

"This is Detective Patterson." he said.

She said, "Yes. This is Sarah."

He said. "Hi. I hope all is well."

Sarah went right into it. She said, "You call me? What is it?" He felt the dislike in her voice, but the detective still remained civil. He said, "Can I come out to your place?"

She said, "What for?"

He said, "You have a manhole on your property, um, following the tide gates charts." He went on to say, "Two homes have them. Yours is one of them."

She sat down on her bed. She suddenly felt as though she had to move her bowels—to be blunt, take a shit. She paused to answer. She firmly said, "No."

"No," he repeated. He said, "No?"

She said, "No."

He said, "May I ask why?"

Then she let him have it. Sarah replied, "The police department is . . . Bullshit, my husband was murdered. And you guys got your head up your ass. Asking all these stupid, fucked-up questions." She said, "Why don't you go find my husband's killer, you asshole." Then she hung up.

The detective paused in thought. Then he tried to call her back. Her phone went to voice mail. He stop for a second and said to himself, *She sounds guilty and is hiding something.* The detective decided to file for a search warrant to go on Sarah property. Little did she know. She called Jazz.

Jazz answered. He said, "Hello."

She said, "Hi."

He said, "Oh, you're up?"

She said, "The detective called me."

Jazz said, "What did he want this time?"

"He wanted to come by and look at the property."

Jazz paused and then said to Sarah, "What did you say?"

Sarah said, "I told him no."

Jazz said, "What did the detective say?"

He asked me why. I just screamed and told him they needed to get their heads out of their ass and find my husband's killer.

Jazz laughed and said, "Really?"

She said, "Yeah."

Jazz said, "OK, keep me posted."

She said, "OK." Then she stood up and later took the kids to the doctor.

Jazz asked why, sounding concerned. But in the back of his mind, he was hoping something had happened to Mikaela. He really wished bad things to happen to her, because he knew she suspected him with her mom. And probably thought he had something to do with her dad's death.

Sarah replied, "I think it will be good for them to hear another person explain about their dad, not just me. And the school—they will see I'm making an effort to help the girls to deal."

Jazz said, "You're right."

He said, "Keep me posted. I have to get back to work."

She said, "OK."

He said, "See you this evening."

She said, "OK."

So after they came from the doctor's office, it was great help. The kids were relaxed with their pediatrician, and they got their thoughts out.

The doctor explained things to them way better than Sarah could ever have. They all cried, and the doctor comforted their thoughts and told them to remember the good things and times that they had with their father.

Sarah took a piece of that therapy for herself for comfort and to try to overcome her guilt.

After the session, they left. They stopped at a fast-food place near the hospital to get a bite to eat. Caitlin asked if they could go to the park, which was close by. They remembered their father bringing them there, chasing them around there.

Sarah said yes.

"When you get through eating, we can go there for a little while." The principal of the girls' school sent Sarah a text to give her love to the girls and said if they both could read a chapter in their history books.

Caitlin was in a lower grade, but she needed to do the same thing too.

Sarah texted the principal back: "OK, and thank you."

Sarah also mentioned to the principal that the girls went to the doctor to talk and that it turned out great and thanked her again for the girls support. The principal texted back with a smiley face.

The phone rang. It was Sarah's boss, saying, "Hoping things are OK."

Sarah said, "It's getting better. Good days, bad days."

He asked Sarah if she was coming to work tomorrow.

Sarah said, "Yes, the girls are doing better. It looks like they can go to school tomorrow."

Sarah's boss said, "That's great. I'm glad they are learning how to cope." He also said, "Tomorrow, there are some people flying in to talk about some advertising project." He said, "It's the same project you have been involved in, and it's almost done. But I need you to stay thirty minutes longer tomorrow. Is that possible?"

Before she could answer, he went on to say, "I'm sorry. I know you have got a lot on your plate. It will just be finished if they can just talk to you about the finishing touches on the project."

Sarah said, "Boss, I understand. I can do it. I will make arrangements with the girls."

Her boss was smiling with joy on the other end, and humbly said thank you.

Then Mikaela called out loud, "Mom!"

Sarah told her, "I'll be right there." Then she told her boss she had to go and she would see him tomorrow."

He said, "OK. Good-bye."

Mikaela wanted Sarah to push them on the swing like she used to do when they were small. They saw the school buses going down the street, and she wanted to get back home before traffic got hectic, so she told the girls, "We are getting ready to leave." And they ran to the car. When they were all inside the car, Sarah told them their principal texted her and said, could they both read chapter 11 in the history books. "That is where the rest of the classes are at in their books." The principal did not want them to fall behind.

The girls stopped in their tracks, and Sarah had their attention while she was telling them about what the principal wanted them to do. They said OK, and when they got home, they went upstairs to their room. Sarah saw that the mail had come. She look through it, but nothing was exciting. She started thinking about Robert. She felt so bad again and felt that if the girls ever found out the truth, they would never forgive her. She went upstairs and turned on the TV and listened to a talk show. Then her phone rang. She knew the number. It was Detective Patterson. She let it go to voice mail, and she played it back. He just said. "Sarah, this is Detective Patterson. Can you please get back to me."

Sarah got angry and deleted the message. She had no intention of calling him back. As the day went on, late afternoon came upon them, and she made beef stew for dinner, and the girls came downstairs perfectly to eat. They had just got through reading chapter 11 in their schoolbooks. The beef stew aroma flowed throughout the house as they were eating.

Jazz came in and said, "Wow. Sarah, that smells so good." He walked quickly through the house. Jazz said, "HI, girls," and then he went upstairs, washed up, and then came down and eat. Sarah made him a bowl. He sat down to eat.

The girls were finishing, but Mikaela said, "Mom, can I have that ice cream for dessert you bought the other day?"

Sarah said, "Why, Mikaela, I thought you forgot about it."

She said, "No, but I really want some."

Now Caitlin said, "Me too."

Sarah said, "OK, OK."

Mikaela glanced at jazz eating, and then Sarah blotted out Mikaela and Caitlin. They said, "Yes, Mommy."

Sarah said, "Tomorrow, I'm going to be a little late picking you up, so I want you to start walking on Main Street, just like Mommy drove, and I will meet you."

Mikaela said, "Why, Mommy?"

Sarah said, "I have to do something at work for a little while longer."

Caitlin was happy. She liked walking with her big sister down the street. Jazz started eating slowly, listening to every word Mikaela said. "OK," Sarah said. "Don't worry, I'll get you. I will pick you up princess."

Mikaela said, "OK, Mommy. I can do it."

"Yes! You can, my big girl."

Mikaela smiled. They finished their ice cream and then went upstairs. They said, "Thank you, Mommy."

Sarah said, "Get dressed for bed, but you can watch TV or play games for only thirty minutes, OK."

They said, OK."

Jazz was eating, and Sarah joined him. She was looking at him eating and said, "You're really hungry, huh." She smiled as he looked at her.

Mikaela came around the corner and had seen them both. Mikaela said, "Mommy, can I wear my light jacket tomorrow? It's supposed to be warm."

Sarah exhaled and said, "Yes, Mikaela. You can wear your light jacket." Then she left.

Jazz said, "See, Sarah. She said what?" He said, "I told you she don't like me, I think she knows."

Sarah said, "Know what?"

He said, "I think she thinks I like you."

She smiled and said, "You do."

Then he said, "I'm serious."

She said, Relax. I'm just getting them to calm down, and here come you.

Sarah just shook her head and said, "I'm going to bed. I have a busy day ahead. Good night."

He said, "Good night."

The evening went quick, and morning came. Sarah got up a little earlier than usual. She wanted to look nice for her job because she was trying to finish the advertising project for the guy who had never seen her that she made the deal with over the phone. The kids got up, ate breakfast, and Sarah piled them in the car as well; and out the door they went.

Jazz woke up. He knew his routine well. Mikaela was on his mind, though he didn't like people knowing his suspicions. Mikaela just didn't like him since her dad was not around. She wanted her dad around her mom, and only her dad. Jazz realized that everyone was gone and that the house smelled like Sarah's perfume scent lingering after she had left.

The girls arrived at school. Sarah said, "Mikaela, remember, Mommy will be a little late. Wait for Caitlin to come out of class and walk straight down Main Street. I will meet you and see you guys are walking and pick you up, OK." They got out of the car. Sarah said, "I love you. Have a good day."

They said, "I love you too, Mommy." As Caitlin and Mikaela were walking, Mikaela said, "Caitlin, don't leave. Wait for me, OK."

Caitlin said, "OK, stop yelling."

Mikaela said, "Hey, Caitlin, Jazz seems to have gotten mean."

Caitlin said, "What do you mean?"

Mikaela said, "He's quiet, and he seems to whisper to Mommy a lot."

Caitlin said, "I don't know, Mikaela. I just miss Daddy so much. But like the doctor said, I'm going to think about the good things we did, like he gave me a piggyback ride."

Mikaela said, "Yeah." Then she added, "See you later. I love you, stinky butt."

Caitlin said, "I love you too, stinky."

And they both went to the class. They called each other nicknames sometimes.

Meanwhile, Detective Patterson was talking to the DA to get a search warrant for Sarah's property. The DA was skeptical to ask the judge because of the public knowing who they were, and they did not talk to get around to thinking the wife was a suspect, but Detective Patterson went on to explain that she got highly upset and accused the police department of not doing the right thing, that some evidence and her objectiveness and guilt made the detective very suspicious of her.

The DA said, "OK, I will go with you on convincing the judge to grant the search warrant. I want to keep this low key."

Detective Patterson said, "You're right."

They both supported each other in convincing the judge, and they were successful.

Jazz was now at work. Things were slow. It's been slowing down since the death of Robert. Anyway, Jazz was aware of Mikaela walking home and picking up Caitlin. He contemplated going up to the school and approaching Mikaela before she picked up Caitlin to see how much she knew. He decided to put a sign up at the store, and it read, "Closed. Be back in 2 hours."

He hustled to the school. It would be getting out shortly, and he didn't want to seem out of breath to bring attention to himself. After all, he was a black African American being at a predominantly white school. He got there, and he assumed it was the big door in the middle. He stood near some cars as though one of them was his, but really not. The door opened, and the kids dispersed. The kids fluttered. The door made it extremely hard for Jazz to see Mikaela, but Mikaela finally came out. She hopped up on the stair banister so Caitlin could see her.

Jazz also spotted her. He walked toward her like a lion going after their prey for food, for her cubs. Mikaela was daydreaming, just watching everyone. All of a sudden, she saw this black guy in her eyes. She focused and now realized it was Jazz. Her heart was beating in her ears, so loud and fast she was frozen. She didn't know what to do. Her legs felt light under her, and trembling, she frantically decided to jump down and blend in the crowd and walk quickly away from the front door.

Jazz was zeroing in on her every move and was getting closer to her. She went on the other side of the crowd and started walking away from school. Jazz stopped as if he was asking himself, *Where is she going?* He wanted to yell, "Mikaela!" But he thought it would draw attention, so he sped his steps up.

Mikaela was crying, jogging a little, trying to get away now. She was a good block away from the school. Caitlin's class was about to come out the same door. Cars were angle-parked on Main Street. No adult were around, although there were cars everywhere. These two cleaning vans were parked beside each other. Mikaela stopped breathing so hard. She was running out of options of what to do, even too tired to scream because she saw Jazz like a shark in the water, not saying a word. He was coming straight at her. Mikaela looked in between the two cleaning vans across the street. To the other direction was a police car. She was so happy she thought she was seeing things. She felt at peace.

Jazz had no idea what she was about to do or say. He knew she had gone in between the vans. He doubled up his footsteps. She looked and saw his body. She turned back and dashed across the street to get the police when she stepped out between the vans 1701 and articulate bus operated in 1899 coming down the street. Henry Rodriguez had been on the job for twenty-five years; he was retiring next month and he was having a beautiful day. All he saw was a four- to five-foot person stepping out less than five feet away from the from him. He hit the brakes and screamed.

Her body hit the right side of the bus. She bounced off the bus and hit two parked cars, nearly touching the third one. He looked to his right, and he noticed a black man, who turned around and went the other way. Henry was frozen. With dry mouth, he picked up the bus radio.

He said, "Emergency, emergency."

Dispatch said, "Go ahead with your emergency."

Henry said. "This is operated 1899. I just made contact with a pedestrian. I am on 1529 Main Street. I need an ambulance, police, and an inspector. The pedestrian appears to be a child. Please come quick."

Dispatch said, "Help is on the way. Stay on the bus."

The police got there in minutes. Right behind them was an ambulance; and Inspector Henry was a wreck. He had tears in his eyes from breathing fast and trembling.

Jazz sprinted back to the store soaked and wet with sweat. He was also shaking, and his mouth was so dry he needed water. He ran the water in the bathroom. He kept hearing sirens blaring, feeling as though everyone was the result of his action.

The EMT paramedic worked frantically on Mikaela. Her little body was broken up so bad; her skull was fractured. Her arms and leg were fractured, and she was bleeding from the eyes.

The cop that was across the street that Mikaela had seen, which caused her to get hit by the bus, was the same officer who told Henry to open the door. Henry did, and the cop said to Henry, "Are you OK?"

Henry said, "Yes. She came from between the vans. Then I slammed on the brakes."

The cop said, "Hang in there. I need to ask you a few questions. Is that OK?"

He said yes.

Then the cop said, "Can you tell me what happened?"

He said, "I was out of service, traveling down the street. She came out from between the vans, and I made contact with her with the right side of the bus."

The EMT knocked on the door to talk to the cop. Henry stepped off the bus for a second. Then he returned to the bus and asked the cop what the EMT said. The cop told him she was dead.

Henry broke down terribly. The cop tried to console him. Then Henry said, "There was a guy behind her."

The cop said, "What?"

Henry repeated it.

The cop said, "Are you sure?"

Henry said, "Yeah, I thought he was with her."

The cop said, "Do you see him around?"

Henry scanned the area quickly with his eyes, because the traffic was building as well as people. He said no.

The cop took the info and told him to call his company, because they needed to tow the bus for further investigation, and he would have to take a drug and alcohol test. Henry said, "No problem."

The officer left to talk to the homicide detective.

Sarah got through at work. The advertising people were pleased with her work. She finalized the deal with the company and actually only had to stay fifteen minutes later. She did not need the whole thirty minutes that her boss told her she needed. She was happy, and the day was going fine. Little did she know she would never be the same once news of the tragedy reached her ears. She got over to the school quickly and planned on making the girls happy when she saw them. She was thinking, *They are growing up*, and knew she had to try to make them happy to hide her guilt and to at least make them successful individuals. She knew Robert would have liked to see this and would be thankful. As she was driving, she noticed that traffic had gotten really intense; but she managed to get all the way to the school. Then she realized that Mikaela and Caitlin did not stick out in her passing.

Sarah almost sideswiped a parked car by scanning so hard to find them. Before she knew it, she was approaching the school, totally baffled. She did not see them. Sarah's heart was beating fast as she wondered things that could have happened. Sarah remembered she had the number of Mikaela's girlfriend Tabitha. She looked down in her purse but had to look up to go around the circle at the school parking lot. She was going around. She saw Caitlin, and her heart started beating fast. Sarah started frantically blowing her horn.

Caitlin turned around and ran down the school stairs. Sarah got out of the car and approached Caitlin with anxiety in her voice. "Where is your sister?"

Caitlin said, "I don't know, Mommy."

She had left her car in the turnaround circle, and she grabbed Caitlin's hand and ran back up the stairs and rang the school bell. The school was quiet. She kept ringing it second after second. Caitlin was getting ready to say everyone's gone, Mommy, but she told Caitlin to be quiet in the middle of her sentence. The bell was still ringing. Finally, she heard the door. The big brass-hinged handle open it. It was a janitor.

Sarah said, "Are there any kids in the school?"

He said, "No, everyone's gone."

She said, "What about the office?"

He said, "It's locked."

Sarah yelled, "Oh! Now where is my baby?" She turned around and took Caitlin's hand, and they went back to the car.

She's started driving she's thinking to drive the same way she told Mikaela to walk. But she was driving at a slow pace. She didn't want to miss any sight that could indicate it was Mikaela. Two blocks away, she was approaching a massive traffic problem. She saw flashing lights and fire trucks and an ambulance. She was going to turn around and take a side street, but she had to stay on the path to clear her mind of her daughter walking as a few people passed her walking. She examined them carefully, praying and wishing it was Mikaela.

Sarah was getting frustrated traffic was going so slow. Even Caitlin was focusing out the window, hoping she would see her big sister. As they got closer to the scene, Sarah could see the officer directing traffic—foot pedestrians and vehicles. One of the kids who was walking with her mom saw Caitlin in the car. The girl yelled, "Hi, Caitlin."

Caitlin looked quickly. Sarah did too. Caitlin smiled. It was one of her classmates. Caitlin said, "HI, Cindy."

Sarah asked Cindy's mom, "What happened up there? The traffic is so slow."

Cindy's mom had tears in her eyes. She said, "A little girl is dead up there. She got hit by a bus."

Sarah said, "Oh my God."

With tears in Cindy's mom eyes, they kept walking. Caitlin said bye to Cindy as well. Traffic continued to flow. Sarah had a focused, concerned look on her face. She was feeling a way she never felt before. As her vehicle's wheels continue to rotate slowly, Caitlin was still staring around. She saw a backpack, and she was saying to herself, *My sister has one.* Then Caitlin see the little doll on the backpack like a key chain in the color of it pink. Caitlin screamed, "Mommy!"

Sarah jammed her foot on the brakes, because the way Caitlin screamed, she knew it had something to do with Mikaela. She said, "What, Caitlin? What, Caitlin?"

"I see Mikaela's backpack."

Sarah said frantically, "What!" Sarah aggressively pulled the car over.

Caitlin said, "Right there, right there!"

Sarah saw it, and she yelled, no! My baby!"

She saw a yellow triangle plastic number card with the number 6 on it. Her breathing got short, and Caitlin said, "What's wrong, Mommy?" And Caitlin started to cry.

Sara opened the door and was ready to dash out of the car. She pulled over and put her four-way flashers on. Then she turned to Caitlin and yelled at her, "Caitlin! Stay in the car! And don't you move at all, do you hear me! Caitlin!"

Caitlin was crying and said, "Yes, Mommy."

Sarah said, "I'm rolling up the windows to a crack. Do not open the door or roll down the window for no one but me, do you understand!"

Caitlin was crying, saying, "Yes, Mommy." Caitlin realized what her mother was thinking. Sarah finally got out. She told Caitlin, "Lock the doors." Sarah started walking quickly, looking left to right. It was crowded with people. She pushed her way through aggressively, slightly saying, "Excuse me." She finally got to the front, where she saw a yellow caution tape and a police officer guarding the crowd. They were all staring at the scene. The people wished the police would pull back the sheet that was covering the child. When Sarah scanned the area, she too spotted a white sheet draped over the child's body, and she saw more of the yellow plastic triangles that displayed numbers on each one as she continued to scan the crime scene area with her eyes. Her heart was beating loudly in her ears. She saw what looked like a familiar shoe. Mikaela. She quickly and aggressively moved her body horizontally to the left.

The people are saying, "Lady, watch it!" People were staring at her. As Sarah's eyes zoomed in on the shoe with the small yellow triangle number, she screamed, "No! No!" Crying, she went through the yellow police caution tape as she was running toward the body. The police quickly grabbed her around her arm in stride. She snatched her arm out of his grip, focusing solely on the blanket sheet. The police hustled a few feet in front of her and placed his body and held his arms out to block her.

She yelled at him, crying, "Get out of my fucking way! That's my daughter."

He said, "Are you sure?"

She was saying, "Move out of my way."

Another police officer saw his colleague in confrontation with Sarah and asked him, "What's going on?"

He said to his fellow officer, "She thinks this is her child."

Both officers looked at each other like, *Oh fuck!* The first officer said, "Ma'am, I will take you over there, but you got to stop being hostile."

She was crying, but she calmed herself down. They slowly started walking toward the party. The homicide officer asked the two officers, "What are they doing?"

They explained to him that Sarah thought this was her child. The detective said to her, "Is your child a girl or a boy?"

Sarah said, "A girl, asshole. Now let me near her."

The detective only asked to make sure she knew what she was going to see. As they were walking, she started to cry, saying, "She was supposed to meet me at the school. She wasn't there."

The detective knew it was her. Now all three officers were trying to be more sympathetic, because they knew what was about to happen.

Then came to the body, and the medical examiner was also there. They were getting ready to remove the body and bring it to the morgue. The detective told the officers to raise the sheet.

Sarah's heart was beating so fast as the officer raised the sheet. Sarah screamed. She kept screaming. The detective grabbed her and held her as she was crying terribly. It was so sad. The officers were feeling her grief. A few had children her daughter's age.

Sarah kept saying, "No, no, no. No, God, no." She was screaming and crying. The officers brought her over to the side. The coroner began to pick up Mikaela's body to put it on the stretcher to bring her to the morgue. Sarah was leaning against the patrol car, and she just kept crying.

The detective said, "You were going to pick her up?"

She said, "Yes."

"So why was she so far from the school? Did she know you were going to pick her up?"

She said, "Yes."

The detective felt there was more, and the girl was dead, so she could tell him why she left the school.

Meanwhile, Caitlin was crying because she felt the dead child Cindy's mother told her mom about was Mikaela. One of the officers that was near Sarah asked the officer with her if he could talk to him for a second. He stepped about three feet away from Sarah, where she was leaning on the car. The officer looked at the other officer and said, "What's up?"

The officer said, "There's a little girl in a car crying, and her doors are locked, and she will not open the doors."

The other officer asked him, "How far is the car?"

"About thirty feet away from the crime scene."

The detective came and joined the two officers' conversation. The detective said to them, "What's wrong?"

They told him, and the detective looked at Sarah and asked her, "How did she get here?"

She said, "My car."

The detective said, "Is there a child in there?"

Sarah's eyes grew big, and she said, "Yes. What's wrong? What's wrong? That's my other daughter, Caitlin."

He said, "She is crying, and the people are concerned, and the doors are locked."

Sarah quickly started walking back to the car. Mikaela's body had already been removed from the crime scene. She stopped and turned back to look at the crime scene one more time and then proceeded to walk to her vehicle. The detective and the officers were walking behind her. Sarah approached her car.

The detective called her name out loud, "Sarah!"

She stopped, turned around, and the detective told her he and the officers would get her away from the crowd. "He will be in front and the other officer will be in the back until you arrive to your property." The detective went on to say, "We want to make sure you get home safely."

Sarah gave him a soft smile that said, *Thank you.* He opened her door, and she got in. They put the lights on. Sarah saw the lights as they made a way for her as if she was the president or a famous person leaving an area.

When Sarah got in her car, Caitlin was crying, "Mommy, was it Mikaela? Was it my sister?"

Sarah said, "Caitlin, put your seat belt on."

Caitlin was crying and said, "Mommy, answer me."

Sarah started crying, "Put your seat belt on, Caitlin."

Caitlin continued to yell and cry terribly. Sarah began driving, following the police escort. Caitlin continue to cry, so Sarah said, "Princess, I'll tell you more when we get home, OK. Mommy is driving, and I have to stay focused because the police are helping us to get home."

Caitlin's crying turned to sniffling, and she said, "OK, Mommy."

They arrived home fairly quickly. The escort helped out a lot. She pulled in the driveway, and she stepped out.

The two officers and the detective approached Sarah. The detective gave her his card and said, "This is an investigation. I will keep you posted on everything, I promise you."

She said, "Thanks." She started to walk to her door, and the detective called out to her. "Sarah!"

She turned around, and he said, "Was there a guy with your daughter?"

Sarah was taken back. She said, "No!"

The detective said, "The bus driver who struck her mentioned he saw someone near her."

Sarah looked concerned and said, "<u>No, no</u> one should be near her. I was the only one who was going to pick her up, and I failed."

He said, "Don't blame yourself. I will keep you informed with the investigation."

She said, "Thank you."

He said, "Try to have a nice evening."

Sarah said, "Thank you."

Caitlin was hugging her tightly by the waist. Sarah turned and walked toward her front door, put the key in the door, and walked in. Caitlin started crying. Sarah too. They held each other tight. Caitlin said she didn't want to go to her room. Sarah said, "You can stay in my room, princess. You can sleep with me."

Caitlin was happy inside, but she continued to cry. She said, "Mom, I need Mikaela. I can't be here without my big sister."

Sarah just held her tight. She was feeling so bad, and she felt bad for Caitlin. She felt as though she was failing. She thought her life was fading away. She was deciding in her mind to send Caitlin to Robert's sister up north. Sarah was thinking to eventually sell the house, sell the store, and start over. She told Caitlin to lie in her bed and that she had to make a phone call. Sarah got up, turned on the TV, grabbed the phone, and went in the living room. She dialed Robert's sister Megan's number.

Megan said, "Hello."

Sarah said, "This is Sarah. How are you?"

Meghan said, "Hi, sis. How are you doing?"

Sarah said, "Not that good." And then she started crying.

Megan said, "What's wrong?"

She said, "I got some bad news to tell you." Sarah was crying as she said, "Mikaela has died."

Meghan said, "What? Oh my God!" She started crying. She said, "How did she die?"

She ran out in the street in front of a bus. The bus killed her. They are doing an investigation now." Meghan was crying. Sarah said, "Can I ask you a favor?"

Meghan said, "What is it?"

Sarah said, "Caitlin's taking it hard. Can she stay with you? I just want to get her away from here. It's too much for her. I got a lot of thinking to do, and I will keep you posted on the funeral."

Meghan said, "Sure. I'll come get her tomorrow."

Sarah was crying as she said, "Thank you so much."

Meghan said, "I'll call you when I am on my way."

Sarah said, "OK. Thank you." They both hung up, and Sarah went back to her bedroom. She was holding Caitlin. This was comforting to Caitlin because she knew her mom was the only one she had. Sarah blamed herself for not picking them up. She would never forgive herself. She felt it was her fault that Mikaela was dead.

She heard the front door. It was Jazz. She got up, closed her bedroom door, because Caitlin had cried herself to sleep. Sarah met Jazz at the door. She just soaked his shirt up with tears, crying in his arms.

He said, "What's wrong?"

She said, "Mikaela is dead."

He said, "Oh my God. What did—when did this happen?"

She said, "Today. It's my fault. I wasn't there to pick them up. Something happened, and she ran in front of a bus. The bus hit her and killed her." She started crying and said, "It's my fault."

Jazz said, "Sarah, it's not your fault. You didn't know." He just held her. He was scared. He knew no one would believe him. He was glad no one knew. Or so he thought.

She said, "I'm sorry I didn't cook."

Jazz said, "It's OK. I'm not hungry."

Sarah said, "Me either. Caitlin is asleep in my bed."

Jazz said, "I'll be in my room, OK."

She said, "OK," and went to her bedroom. Sarah fell asleep.

No one had dinner. Jazz was stressed. He was so nervous thinking someone seen him. Caitlin and Sarah continued to sleep through the remainder of the night.

Daytime came quickly. Caitlin was starting to wake up. Sarah said, "Princess, you can sleep longer. You are staying home with me."

Caitlin said, "OK."

Sarah lay down with her daughter. Caitlin kept her eyes closed. She was so sad knowing she wouldn't be playing with her sister ever again. Meanwhile, Jazz was waking up. He walked to the bathroom. He took a quick shower and then went back to his room. He got dressed and immediately left. He wanted to get far from the house.

Robert's sister called Sarah. She told Sarah, "Hi, I know it's early, but I'm on my way to pick up Caitlin."

Sarah said, "OK. She will be ready."

Caitlin said. "Mommy, who was that?"

She said, "Auntie Megan. You are going to be with her for a while."

Caitlin said, "What about you?"

She said, "Princess, I will be there. I got to make arrangements for your sister, and I have to wait for the report."

Caitlin started crying, saying, "Don't leave me please!"

Sarah said, "Caitlin, don't you like Auntie Megan? It would be better for you if you don't have to go to school here. I will take care of things here. Then I will be up."

Caitlin shook her head in agreement. Sarah went to Caitlin's room to get her things ready for Meghan. Her cell phone rang. She looked and saw it was the police. She didn't pick up. She couldn't deal with any talk about Mikaela, and she definitely didn't want to speak to Detective Patterson. She played back the voice mail.

It was Detective Patterson, calling to given his condolences for Mikaela. He said, "Detective Durant is handling her case. But if you need me as well, please contact me at this number." Then he said he would try one more time to talk to her about her property. About Robert.

Sarah deleted the message. She told Caitlin, "Put some clothes on before your Auntie Meagan gets here."

Jazz just got to the store. He was angry when he got there. The shelves were getting empty, and money needed to be deposited in the bank. Sarah was the only one who had the power to do both, and she hadn't done anything. Jazz, in a way, wanted to say "Fuck it" and leave everything. But that would only cause more suspicion.

Auntie Meghan arrived at the house. Sarah hugged her tight.

Megan said, "It's OK, Sarah. Robert's family is here for you. You will be fine. It just takes time."

Caitlin came into the living room where they were standing. Megan hugged her tight. Caitlin started crying, and Meghan was crying too. She said, "I'm sorry, princess. Auntie Meghan will help you get through this."

It was just hugs and tears from everyone for about five minutes. Sarah said, "I will walk you guys to the car." They all stepped out of the house and walked to Megan's car. Sarah said, "Put your seat belt on, Caitlin." Sarah gave Meghan a hug and said, "Thank you so much."

Megan told her she loved her and that Caitlin would be fine. She got in the car and then backed out of the driveway and drove off. Sarah watch until the car was out of sight.

Detective Duran was still interviewing Henry Rodriguez, the bus driver who struck and killed Mikaela. All his tests came back negative. And he was still looking at the mugshots book. After ninety-seven pages in the book, he found a guy that he swore was behind Mikaela. He grabbed the book and poked his head out the door of the interview room. He saw Detective Durant and said, "Detective, can I see you for a minute."

Detective Durant broke away from the conversation he was having with the officer and walked back into the interview room to talk to Henry. The detective said, "Yes, Henry, what's up?"

Henry said, "I see the man that was with Mikaela, or I think it is."

Detective Durant said, "Show me."

Henry said, "Him—the black guy."

Detective Durant looked at the picture and then looked at Henry. He said, "Are you sure?"

Henry said, "I am quite sure this was the guy."

Detective Durant also told Henry that all his tests came back negative. After he ID'd the guy, Detective Durant told him that he was free to go, but that he would keep him posted if he had any questions.

Henry said, "OK. And thank you."

Detective Durant told him to hang in there—it appeared to be just a tragic situation. Henry shook the detective's hand and left the police station. Detective Durant took the info off the mugshot of the person that Henry picked out. Later, he got a hit on the information. The guy was Jazz St. Jean, 3229 Raspberry Lane. It was the same address as Mikaela's.

He immediately called Sarah. It went to voice mail, so he left her a message to call him back. He decided to go by her house, hoping she was home. After all, she had just lost her child. She was in no shape to face her job. He wanted to see Detective Patterson before he went to Sarah's house to let him know what he had discovered, if he didn't already know.

But Detective Patterson wasn't in his office. So Detective Durant left to head to Sarah's house. When he got there, the house was quiet, but her car was in the driveway. He rang the bell a good five times.

She looked through the side window, and she noticed a police cruiser. She was getting her mind and building her anger to give Detective Patterson a piece of her mind. She was in no mood to hear this Robert's mystery death shit. But she looked through the door, and she saw it was not him. It was detective Durant. Her whole expression immediately changed, and eagerness took over. She opened the door and said, "Hi."

He said, "Hi."

She said, "Come in."

He stepped inside the house. She further told him to have a seat in the living room. He had a serious look on his face, and she had a concerned look on hers. He went on to say that the bus driver who hit and killed Mikaela ID'd the guy who he thought was following her. Sarah was staring in the detective's eyes and lips and couldn't wait to hear who it could be, if anybody. She said, "Have you questioned him?"

Detective said, "Well, no. That's another reason why I'm here." He asked, "Does a gentleman named Jazz St. Jean live here?"

She was silent for a second, and then shocked. She was still staring in his eyes. She finally answered, "Yes. Yes, he does."

Detective Durant said, "Really? That's who the bus driver ID'd."

Sarah said, "What! Are you sure?" She was thinking, *This can't be true.* She turn and walked away from him and said, "Detective, all due respect, it's impossible. He worked at the hardware store we own, so I can't even imagine where you got this information." Sarah was slowly getting angry. She was losing all faith in law enforcement.

Detective Durant said, "Ma'am, I would like to question him. Is he here now?"

She said, "No. He is at work."

He said, "I won't go to the store, but have him call me. I would like to have a talk with him at the station."

Sarah said, "You want him to come to the station?"

He said, "Yes."

She said, "OK, I will definitely see to it." She said, "Detective, thank you. I just don't feel this is even true, but I have faith you will get to the bottom of it."

He said, "There's a child dead. I don't take this lightly, and if somebody pushed or was chasing her, I will get them. He stood up and said, "I will be in touch, and please give Jazz St. Jean the message and my card."

She said, "I will. And thank you again." She opened the front door, and he walked out. Sarah close the door and had a blank look on her face, with no question or answer. She don't know what to think or do. She picked up the house phone, mainly because she was standing in the living room. She called Jazz. When Jazz answered, she said, "Hi, it's me."

He said, "Hi."

She said, "I need you to close the store. I need to talk to you. It's very important."

Jazz's insides felt like a stone. He said, "Close the store?"

She said, "Yeah. Put a sign on the door, 'Closed today, family emergency.' Everyone knows the family had a tragedy."

He said, "OK."

She hung up, didn't say good-bye or anything. She started thinking and remembering how Jazz was acting days ago. She thought of her daughter, and she said out loud, "Don't worry, princess. Mommy will get to the bottom of it." She lay down. She called the school, and the principal answered. Sarah said, "HI, this is Mrs. McKinley, Caitlin's mom."

The principal said, "Yes, I'm sorry."

Sarah said, "Thank you." Then she said, "Caitlin won't be back for the rest of the year. She just can't handle any more. She is with my sister-in-law up north."

The principal said, "I totally understand. Thanks for calling. Everyone here is praying for your family."

Sarah said, "Thank you," and hung up.

Detective Durant was almost at the police station. He saw Detective Patterson loading up a big SUV, so Durant pulled up beside Patterson.

Patterson said, "What's up?"

Durant said, "Can I talk to you for a quick minute?"

Patterson hesitated to answer. Durant said, "Real quick," and Patterson said, "OK."

Durant got out and said, "I know you heard about the McKinley girl."

Detective Patterson said, "Right?"

Durant said, "Yeah. That's my case. The driver who hit her said he saw someone behind her."

Detective Patterson said, "Really?"

Durant said, "Yeah. He also ID'd him from a mugshot book."

Patterson said, "And?"

"It's a guy, Detective, who lives in her house."

Detective Patterson yelled, "What!"

Detective Durant said, "Yeah."

Detective Patterson said, "Are you sure?"

Durant said, "Yes."

Detective Patterson asked, "Who is it?"

Durant said, "The guy's name is Jazz St. Jean."

Detective Patterson said, "He live there?"

Durant said, "Yeah."

Patterson said, "How long?"

Durant said, "I don't know. He's supposed to be coming in for questioning."

Patterson was surprise and mad. He said, "Sarah never mentioned him in her husband's murder."

"So," Detective Durant said, "where are you going?"

Patterson said, "Funny you should ask. I have a search warrant for Sarah McKinley's property and home."

Detective Durant said, "Why?"

Patterson said, "I asked her kindly, can I look on her property."

Durant said, "Why?"

Patterson said, "There's a tide gate that leads to the ocean on her property and a half a mile away, another house has a drain line on their property. But Sarah's leads to the ocean. And I believe her husband was killed on his property. I just need proof. When I asked her about her property, she told me to fuck off."

Durant laughed.

"So I got the DA involved, and I was able to get a search warrant for the whole premises, internal and external."

Detective Durant said, "Should I come?"

Detective Patterson said, "No. I got a few CSI guys behind me." The detective looked impatient, and Detective Durant said, "OK. If you need me, call me on the radio. I'll be in the office."

Patterson said, "OK."

Durant said, "Be careful." And then he walked toward the police station.

Meanwhile, Sarah patiently waited for Jazz. She called the store to see that he had left. The phone just rang, so she knew he was on his way. She looked out the window. It was only the letter carrier throwing mail through her mail slot. She walked away.

Minutes later, she heard car doors closing one right after another. She walked back to the window. There were three police cars. One car and two SUVs blocked out Detective Patterson heading up the walkway. Sarah was pissed off. Detective Patterson was heading up the walkway. He saw her car in the driveway. He rang the bell. He said, "Sarah," and before he could finish, she opened the door and just stared at him. He said, "Sarah, I have a search warrant to search your property and your house."

She rolled her eyes up into the ceiling and said, "What possibly could you be looking for?"

He said, "I don't know. Why don't you tell me."

She said, "Fuck you." And walked away and sat on the couch.

He laid the search warrant on the table and went back outside. He instructed the officers to look for anything—"a shoe print, broken objects, and if you find a manhole cover, let me know."

They all said, "OK" and went to work looking for clues.

Sarah called Jazz to let him know to stall coming home.

One of the officers yelled, "Detective!"

Patterson walked toward him. The officer pointed down. He had found the manhole. Detective Patterson noticed the ground was really moist, like it had rained or flooded. The officer who found it asked, "How do you get this open?"

Patterson looked around the yard and told the officer that was approaching him, "Can you look in the garage for something to lift this? It should have a hook on it like a hanger type, but heavier."

The officer said, "OK."

Patterson knew Sarah would not volunteer any assistance. The officer looked in the garage, his eyes rotating around the wall to the floor. He noticed the girls' bikes, some garden tools, and a three-foot metal hook. He grabbed it and gave it to Detective Patterson. The office was smiling as he walked over. Detective Patterson said, "So you want to make detective one day," joking with him. Detective Patterson stuck the metal hook in the manhole, and he noticed the cover was extremely heavy. He felt it move, and he struggled to take it off, but he got it off. The officer had a flashlight. He whipped it out and shone it down the manhole. There was total darkness, and everyone was quiet. Detective Patterson smirked and said to himself, *Robert, talk to me. Tell me what happened.*

Detective Patterson was looking to piece things together. He and all the officers heard the water rushing down plain as day. And the hole below was huge; it was a small car park down there. Detective Patterson was contemplating bringing Sarah in for questioning; but he didn't want to jump the gun. He took pictures of the manhole. He said, "OK, boys, closed this up, and we are going to march and do the same thing inside."

One of the officers took some pictures too and took the hook from Detective Patterson and slid the cover back on top of the manhole. He made sure it was secured to the manhole.

Sarah saw them coming to her front door again. She was nervous; she didn't know what he was going to say. Detective Patterson led the way to the front door. He was getting ready to ring the bell, but she opened the door. He had a soft, serious look on his face as he said to her, "The search warrant I gave you also gave me permission to search your house inside."

She said, "What the fuck are you looking for, asshole?"

He looked her in the eyes and said, "I don't know, but if you could tell me what I should be searching for, I would appreciate it." Detective Patterson said, "Sarah, I don't believe Robert was killed outside his home."

She said, "Oh, you think I did it?"

He said, "Is this a confession?"

She said, "Fuck you."

He said, "Move out of the way."

Sarah took two steps to the side.

Detective Patterson filed in inside along with six other officers. He instructed some officers to take the upstairs. Two to look on the main floor and two could do the basement. Detective Patterson was taking pictures of the inside of the house. Sarah picked up her cell phone and tried to tell Jazz not to come home <u>yet.</u>

<u>As</u> his phone was ringing, Jazz was walking down the street, almost at the house; but he noticed black SUVs and unmarked cruisers in front of the house. His heart was beating fast; he was thinking they would think he killed Mikaela and was looking for him. He turned and started walking in the other direction right back down the street. He look at his cell phone and noticed it was Sarah. He didn't pick up the phone. He was thinking the cops were making her call him to catch him, but she was merely trying to tell him, "Don't come home."

Sarah walked back into the living room. Detective Patterson was watching all her moves out of the corner of his eye. All the officers had on blue surgical gloves, including Detective Patterson. They came from downstairs with several plastic evidence bags and quietly talked to Detective Patterson to tell him what they had found. He ordered them to put the bags in their truck, and then the officer upstairs came downstairs with one bag, and the officer on the first floor took some pictures and a knife back in the kitchen that was on the wall. There were a few handles they saw near the kitchen door like shovel handles.

Sarah was worried, but still remaining calm, she told Detective Patterson, "When am I going to get back my belongings back?"

He said, "The police department will send you a copy of a letter explaining when they will bring these items back." Then he walked away and then turned back around to say, "If these items turn out to be nothing."

Sarah gave him the middle finger. Truly, these two were not friends and would not be receiving Christmas cards from each other. She watched them get in the vehicles and leave, and then she quickly walked around the house to see what was missing. The plastic bags the officers had. She couldn't see through them. She noticed Detective Patterson had left a paper on the coffee table. It was her copy of the list of the items they took, with his signature at the bottom. She went to the kitchen. She noticed the knives were missing. The cabinet drawers were open, and the downstairs door leading to Robert's office was open. She took a few steps down there, and she noticed a baby-blue liquid. She tried to smell it, but it contained no scent. It was a substance that police use to track blood. If it lit up, that means there are traces of blood.

Sarah hadn't really put all this together yet. Her mind was boggled with so much. But little did she know that she was fucked. She walked back upstairs and locked the door.

Jazz had seen the black SUV fly by, so he hustled into the house, hoping Sarah was still there. He turned the key to the front door to open it. Sarah heard the front and hoped it was Jazz. It was, and she didn't know where to begin, in her mind, to tell him about the search warrant or to question him about Michaela.

Jazz said, "I would have been here sooner, but I saw the police cars down the street."

Sarah said, "I tried to call you, but you didn't pick up."

Jazz said, "I thought they might have put you up to call me." He said, "Why? Why did you call me and tell me to rush home?" He is looking at her suspiciously, like she was setting him up. He was remembering being set up before.

She exhaled and said, "Well, I don't know where to start. OK, I'll start here. Detective Patterson wanted to check for clues on my property. I told him no in the past. He went and got a search warrant, so they searched the property, so that's when you saw them when you were coming here."

Jazz said, "Oh, yeah, I see. I understand."

Sarah paused and then continue, "I called you home for something totally different."

He had a puzzled look on his face and said, "Oh, what is it?"

She went on to say, "Detective Durant—he is investigating Mikaela's death."

Jazz said, "Why? The bus hit her."

She said, "Let me finish, and don't interrupt me."

His eyes got serious, because the tone of her voice had changed. He said, "OK, go ahead. Sorry."

She went on to say that Detective Durant interviewed the bus driver, who stated that he had seen someone behind Mikaela right after he hit her. And Sarah said, "He, the detective, told me it was you."

Jazz's eyes grew big. "Me?"

Sarah said, "Yes, you."

Jazz said, "How can that be?" His heart was beating loud in his ear.

Sarah said, "That's what I said to the detective. Anyways, the police want you to come to the station to talk to them."

Jazz said, "So what did you say?"

I told them you were at work and there was no way that you could have been there."

Jazz calmed down a little. He said, "What did Detective Durant say?"

"He said you've been ID'd, and he still wants to talk to you."

He walked away from Sarah.

Sarah said, "Were you with my daughter?"

Jazz said, "No! I was at work."

She said, "I am going to the store and download the store video."

He said, "Why?"

Sarah said, "For one, to prove to the police you were at the store. Then to prove to myself you were at the store." She grabbed her keys and her sweater.

He said, "Wait!"

Sarah turned around. She had an angry expression on her face.

Jazz tried to have a sympathetic expression. He was thinking he had to tell her because she would see it on the tape that he left early. He said, "Sarah, you got to listen to me."

Sarah was quiet, but she was breathing fast. Jazz started by saying he was going to the school to talk to Mikaela to ask her why she was angry with him.

Sarah said, "You were there?" She was so heartbroken. Her eyes were circling everywhere; a thousand things were going through her mind. The cops were right. The bus driver was right. She was saying these things in a low tone.

Jazz was saying, "No! No! I didn't kill her!"

Sarah said in a loud voice, "Yes you did! You killed my daughter." She turned around and walked toward Jazz, swinging at his face. He is dodging her hands. She said, "You killed my baby Mikaela." She started crying.

Jazz caught her arms. He said, "Stop! This not true! I tried to reach for her, and before you knew it, she dashed in front of the bus."

Sarah said, "Why were you going to see her? She is just a child. My baby. She couldn't hurt you. You scared her. She ran into the street 'cause of you."

He said, "No, that's not true."

Sarah was crying and crying, saying, "Mikaela, I'm sorry, baby. I'm so sorry, baby. Mommy let you down." She was crying hard. She was thinking to herself and finally said out loud, "I got to go to the police." She was walking to door.

Jazz grabbed her and said, "What?" He was getting angry.

She yelled at him, "I'm going to the police! They need to know the story, so I can bury my daughter."

Jazz said, "Stop! Think about what you are saying! They will arrest me!"

She said, "You killed her!"

He said, "No! I didn't!" He was breathing hard. She was too. He was getting angry. Jazz said, "Go ahead, Sarah. Say what you like."

Sarah was shocked. He was looking at her as he said, "If they arrest me, they will also find out you killed your husband."

She looked at him so evil. She was thinking,

He said, "You will be in prison for the rest of your life. You will never see Caitlin."

She was thinking, slowly losing her confidence.

He said, "We are in this together, and it will work, because I'm not going back to prison."

Sarah said, "They will find out."

Jazz said, "No, they won't! You're going to go to the store and disable the video camera. And when the detective asks you about it, you're going to say it's been broken for a while and Robert never got to fix it."

Sarah listened and was shocked by how quickly he put that story together. She was also thinking that if he did that, he definitely had a motive with Mikaela. She was so angry and sad, but she felt helpless in Jazz's clutches that she had to obey his command and his schemes. But knowing he killed her daughter, she was wishing he was dead, and she wanted him dead. She just couldn't think of a way for it to be done. She turned from the front door area and headed to the bedroom door. She had tears in her eyes like a teenage kid who just got grounded.

Jazz had his hands on his hips and dropped his head like, *Damn this is getting hard with Sarah*. But he knew he had to keep an eye on her and keep her under his thumb at all times.

Detective Durant saw Detective Patterson coming back from the McKinley house. Detective Durant said to Patterson, "Wow, you just getting back."

Patterson smiled and said, "Yeah, it was very productive. The CSI officer sprayed luminol in the room downstairs. There was blood was on the floor, like the body was dragged."

Detective Durant said, "Really? Did you see Jazz?"

Detective Patterson said, "Who?"

Durant said, "I told you, he's staying <u>there.</u>"

"No, he wasn't there, and if that was his room in the back, we found nothing. But, Detective Patterson, the kitchen looked like we also may have something."

Detective Durant said, "If you're that confident, why don't you have a warrant for her arrest?"

Patterson said, "I need one more piece of solid evidence, and then I will do just that." Then Patterson said, "What about you?"

Detective Durant said, "I'm giving that guy Jazz St. Jean twenty-four hours. If he does not come here, I will definitely go to him—the house or the job. I definitely think they had enough publicity in respect to Robert McKinley. I'm trying not to go to the store he owned. But he has twenty-four hours to see me. If not, I will be at his door."

Patterson was nodding his head in agreement. He said, "Hey, let me start sorting out this evidence. Wish me luck."

Durant said, "Good luck. Talk to you soon."

Patterson said, "OK, thank you. Talk to you later."

They both went their separate ways in the police station.

Jazz went to his room and got dressed to go to sleep, like he always did, in boxers and a tank top. He was playing light, soft instrumental music, trying to relax. The day running day turning to late evening he is lying down in his bed, with his hands folded behind his head, his window slightly cracked open. He could feel the wind, and the sun looked red in the evening. It looked so nice. He wished things could be good, but for now, he was unwinding and eventually drifting off to sleep. He heard a knock on his door. It was Sarah. She was standing there. She never came down to his room before. His heart was beating fast, and his mouth got really dry he almost couldn't swallow.

She said, "Can I come in?"

He said yes. She had on a Red Sox T-shirt, with the T-shirt being the color red. Her hair was wavy, like she just got out of the shower. Her toes were painted the same color of her T-shirt. Jazz was thinking in his mind she looked like a college girl in a dorm. But he was not really smiling because he knew how her mind had been lately. She was smelling up his room with some kind of shower powder, but the aroma was starting to turn him on. He said to her, "What's wrong?"

She walked to him real close and sat on his bed. She said in a soft voice, "I don't want to be alone in my room. Can I stay in here?"

He said, "Sleep in here?" She nodded her head, saying yes. He scooped her up and whispered in her ear, "You are so beautiful."

She turned her head to his face and started kissing him. His mouth covered hers, with both of his lips touching only her bottom lip. Then he slipped both of his lips to the right side of her neck, inhaling the powder of her fragrance. Her wavy black hair touched his face every time his lips were on the side of her neck. She lifted her head back, and she was looking up at the sky through the window, and tears were running down her face. But she was wiping them secretly as she thought about her daughter Mikaela.

Jazz was so fixated on her skin. He was like a python slithering over its victim. His lips moved to her shoulder, and now in front of her chest, sucking on her pink in color 1/2 in breast nipples. Her C-cup breast was no match for the size of his lips. His penis got harder every time he touched her skin.

She felt as though he was attacking her body, but gently. His lips were now down to her navel. He wanted her vagina in his mouth. The pure, clean scent of her body did not change as he began to kiss her lower. He suddenly realized she had no panties on when she entered his room, knowing what she was going to allow him to do. He relaxed in his mind because he wanted to enjoy this and express his feelings to her, not just cum inside her, but to show and demonstrate to her how her body should be worshiped. He was licking her bald vagina like a wounded animal. She was starting moan, which was turning him on. She as palm his bald head. She was putting his head in the area where she wanted his lips to kiss. She put her hands on his head without saying a word, just having his lips and tongue constantly moving. Even Robert never did it this good. She was enjoying it, and her heart was beating so fast because she wanted to release in his mouth so bad, and finally she did. With moaning and yelling, letting him know she was satisfied.

He moved slowly back up to her face, whispering words to her: "I never want you to leave me."

She whispered back, "I won't," as she rubbed her hands all over his dark skin. She kissed him—on his lips and on his chest, rubbing his stomach, feeling how hard his penis was, standing straight up like the Eiffel Tower. She climb on top of him. Jazz was so happy; he opened his eyes to see her pretty face. He never had anyone as pretty and sexy as her. She was putting his penis in her wet vagina, and they both were moaning. She rocked front and back slightly. Hopping up and down on it, feeling his penis almost in her stomach, going faster and harder. Jazz was feeling her slamming down on his groin area; it was so good to him, and he eventually exploded all inside of her. He was holding her waist as she lay on top of his chest, and with his penis still inside her, they both drifted off to sleep.

Detective Patterson was examining every piece of evidence from Sarah's home. Pictures of the outside, pictures inside. The manhole. So far, he was coming up empty. He was still OK because when they sprayed Robert's office in the house downstairs they found blood spatter, and the blood was Robert's. Officer Hathaway was helping with the evidence. He was doing evidence from the kitchen, and he was pretty good at putting the pieces together. He was a good CSI. Detective Patterson felt confident that between the two of them, they would find a crucial piece of evidence. As Hathaway checked the kitchen appliances, mainly the knives, he examined each one carefully, from the point to the handle, the width and the sharpness. He was admiring the fact that the McKinleys had good taste in knives and appliances. They weren't cheap. The Craftsman utensils were top-notch. He came across the one set of a platinum knife case. All those knives had pearl handles. All of them were in sequence, from small, medium, large. As he examined each one, he noticed that one of the metal tips was slightly broken. It was still sharp, and if you looked quickly, it looked perfect play normal. He compared the small one to the medium one, and the medium one to the large one. He did this over and over again for at least twenty minutes. Then he got on the computer and googled the same year and make and model of these pearl-handled knives. Then he focused on the medium one, and he smiled to himself. He was right—there was a piece missing. Now he was hoping he could track down the piece through other evidence.

With his experience, He was aware of a knife breaking on impact when it may strike the victim's bone if the murderer hit the victim with that much force. He took all his findings and went to find Detective Patterson to let him know what he came up with. Hathaway went into Detective Patterson's office. Detective Patterson was in, and Hathaway stood at his door. Patterson waved his hand to signal him to come in, but put his finger over his lips, to be quiet. Patterson was listening to Robert's messages on the cell phone. The cell phone was collected as evidence that Robert was working in his office. Hathaway walked in on Robert's phone, and he heard moaning. Patterson was totally baffled. He couldn't make it out, or why it was there.

There was nothing else on Robert's phone—no sex pictures or anything, no infidelity of any kind. Patterson asked CSI Hathaway, what did he think? y

Hathaway said, "Hmm. Play it again."

Patterson did, and Hathaway said, "Maybe he thought his wife was cheating."

Detective Patterson's eyes got so big and he said in a loud voice, "What did you say!"

Hathaway looked Patterson in the eyes and said, "His wife was cheating on him, and he recorded it. There was a struggle, and she killed him."

They both gave each other the high five, but Hathaway said to Patterson, "But that's not all!" Looking like a clever scientist raising his finger, he then presented the knife.

Detective Patterson said, "Is that the murder weapon?"

Hathaway said, "Ninety-five percent, I think so."

Detective Patterson said, "What's stopping it?"

Hathaway said, "A piece of a knife is missing, and I want to check with the medical examiner to see if there was any foreign metal in the body." Hathaway went to say, "I think when she stabbed him, the knife broke."

Detective Durant came in. He said, "You guys having a party and didn't invite me?"

They laughed. Detective Patterson said, "The McKinley case is coming along." He played the cell phone to Durant. Patterson said, "What do you think of this?"

Durant listened to the message. He said, "No! She was cheating on Robert? With that guy? Jazz?"

Patterson said, "One might think so."

Detective Durant said, "Do you think he killed him? Or was it Sarah?"

Patterson and Hathaway said, "We don't know which one. but one of them is definitely the murderer. So if we arrested one of them, one will tell on the other." Detective Patterson added, "I think it's Sarah."

Durant said, "Why her and not Jazz?"

Patterson said, "Sarah has more to lose, and she tried her best to elude me for a while. I had sympathy for her, but now I realize she is a ruthless killer."

CSI Hathaway and Detective Durant were quiet. Patterson called the DA to let her know what was going on. He was going to arrest Sarah McKinley for the murder of Robert McKinley, her husband.

It was morning, and Sarah woke up in Jazz's bed. Jazz was up already and was in the bathroom. Sarah picked up the T-shirt she had on when she entered his bedroom. She slipped it over her head and went to her bedroom. She lay across her bed; she was feeling so angry. She felt as though her whole life was gone. She grabbed the phone to call Robert's sister, who had Caitlin. She dialed the number, and the call went to voicemail. Sarah left a message saying, "HI, it's me, Sarah. Just wondering how Caitlin is doing. I miss her and need to hear her voice. Please call me when you can. Love you guys." And then she hung up.

Jazz came out of the bathroom and went straight to his room. He noticed Sarah was in there and didn't make his bed. He made his bed before he left to go to work. He peeked in Sarah's door, and he said, "Morning, sexy. I am leaving, OK."

She was laying on her stomach, her back to the door. She responded, "OK, have a good day."

He realized she seemed sad, and he didn't want to say the wrong thing to her, so he just left.

She was so mad, really. But Jazz thought she was OK. He thought she was just having a bad morning. Little did Jazz know she hated him for killing her little girl. Yes, she thought, if he wasn't chasing her, she would be alive today. Robert she could deal with, but Mikaela was helpless, and Sarah felt she should have been there for her. Her phone was on the bed. She was so mad she threw it against the wall.

Ironically, right after she threw it, the phone rang. She couldn't believe it. It was Robert's sister Meghan. Sarah said, "Hello."

Meghan said, "Caitlin called."

She said, "Hi, Mommy."

It was the joy she needed to hear. Caitlin sounded happy. Sarah's eyes filled up with water. Sarah said, "Hi, princess, how are you? Mommy missed you so much."

Caitlin said, "Me too. Auntie Meghan took me to breakfast."

Sarah said, "Really! That must have been really fun."

Caitlin said, "It was. Please come see me, Mommy. I don't want to go there. I can't take it." Caitlin started getting sad.

Sarah said, "Yes, I'm coming soon. Can't wait. And I'm bringing you a surprise." Sarah was trying to cheer her up.

Caitlin said, "Really?"

Sarah said, "Yes, princess."

"Auntie Megan wants to talk to you."

Sarah said, "OK, put her on the phone."

Caitlin said, "I love you, Mommy."

Sarah said, "I love you so much, my princess. Be good for Auntie Megan."

Caitlin said, "I will."

Sarah said, "Put Auntie Megan on the phone."

Caitlin said, "OK." She passed Meghan the phone.

Megan said, "Sorry, we weren't here when you called. We went for breakfast."

Sarah said, "It's OK. Caitlin sounds so happy. Thank you so much."

Meghan asked Sarah, "How are you doing?"

She said, "I'm holding on. Good days, bad days. You know." She added, "They might be releasing Mikaela's body for burial. It's going to be hard, but I'll keep you posted on it."

Meghan said, "OK."

Sarah said, "OK, I'll let you go for now, but thank you so much."

Megan said, "I love you, Sarah."

Sarah said, "I love you too."

They hung up. Although she felt better, she was even angrier at Jazz. She slept with Jazz to let him think things would be fine, but she wanted to kill him. Jazz had no idea about the anger and hate she had for him because of Mikaela's death. Sarah felt she couldn't go on until he was dead; but she knew he would go to the police about Robert's death. And it would be over for her, and she would never see Caitlin again.

The phone rang. It was Jazz. He said, "Hi. I hate to bother you." She was getting even madder when he was talking. She didn't want to listen to his voice, but she had to. She said, "I'm OK."

Jazz said, "You really need to come and take care of this money and take it to the bank. There's like forty thousand dollars here, and I need to order supplies—"

She interrupted him and said, "OK, OK, I'll be there, and I'll call you when I'm on my way."

He said, "Are you sure!"

She put on a fake tone. "Yes, I'm sure." Although he was trying to be rude because she had been ignoring him about the supplies in the store, he wished he could do it all. Then he said, "Bye. Got to go."

A thought came to Sarah's mind—a deviant thought. She thought she could frame both murders on Jazz. Jazz had no idea she was plotting to kill him. And her anger was making it easy because of Mikaela. She went downstairs to Robert's office, where he kept a gun locked in his bottom desk drawer for the store and for the home. She thought if he would have gotten it in her rage with him, he probably would have shot her. She unlocked the drawer, and the gun was still there. She put a clip in it and brought it upstairs. Now she knew what was going to happen. She started getting dressed to go out to the store. She was smiling to herself. *Don't worry, princess. Mommy will get him for taking your life.*

Detective Patterson had made a call to the medical examiner. He said, "Hi, this is Detective Patterson."

The examiner said, "Hi, Detective Patterson, I am just about to ready to close this case, but I need to ask a question."

"OK," Detective Patterson said. "Did you find any fragment or foreign objects or anything that may have broken off into the body?"

The medical examiner said, "Funny that you called. I am closing out my monthly report on the McKinley case. It was one of my interesting autopsies."

Patterson said, "Why is that?"

"I found a piece of metal impaled in the sternum."

Detective Patterson said, "Ouch! That must have hurt."

The medical examiner said, "Obviously. He died of multiple stab wounds and bled out from the puncture. It was right in the heart."

Patterson said, "I see."

The medical examiner paused and said, "I think I have the piece of the murder weapon. I'm quite sure it's the piece. Well, I must tell you it's a small piece and weird in shape."

Patterson was smiling and said, "I'm quite sure that's it." He then went on to say, "I will be there in forty-five minutes, and I will have the other part of the weapon."

The medical examiner said, "OK, I will see you then."

Patterson said, "Thank you," and hung up. He said to himself, *Sarah, I got you.*

Sarah had on jeans and sneakers and had her hair pulled back. She had on a hoodie sweatshirt that had a college logo on it. She was definitely dressed in a physical outfit. She put the gun in her purse and left the house and got in the car and drove off. She had confidence because she knew that this had to be done. She was driving, and she was just as calm as she could be. You would think she would second-guess herself. She approached the store, and she saw Jazz waiting on a customer. She slowly pulled the car into the spot. She got out of the car. She put her bag over shoulder and started walking into the store.

Jazz glance up and saw her, and he was saying to himself, *Wow! She came like she said.*

Little did he know this would be the last time he would see her or the store.

Detective Patterson arrive at the medical examiner's office. He asked to speak to the medical examiner. He said, "I am Detective Patterson."

The medical examiner said, "Can I see the weapon?"

Patterson said, "Sure." They walked a few steps, made a right turn around the corner to a place that appeared to be a lab. He went into his file drawer, and Detective Patterson noticed the small plastic bag. It had Robert's name on it and some number. The medical examiner placed it over the silver tray. He opened the little plastic bag. A metal piece slid out onto this stainless steel tray. Patterson's eyes were glued to the whole process. The medical examiner picked up the tiny piece with what appeared to be tweezers. He took the knife, which was the other part of the weapon, and slid it into the broken gap of the knife. They fit like a lock and a key.

Patterson smiled and yelled, "Yes!" And he did held his hand up like an umpire would do at a baseball field making a call. The medical examiner took a picture of the perfect fit and then placed the small piece back in the small plastic bag. He quickly filled out a form and handed it to Detective Patterson.

Patterson sign it, and then the medical examiner signed it. He said, "Good job." Patterson headed back to the police station to put it in the evidence room. He knew now he had enough evidence to arrest Sarah for the murder of her husband.

Sarah entered the store and wave at the customers. She continued to walk to the back of the store where the store office was. She hadn't been in there for a while. She was looking around as though it was her first time in there. She saw the picture that Robert hung up in there of her and the girls. She opened the safe, and a whole bunch of bills wrapped came rolling out. Jazz was right. It wasn't full. He kept the money neat like Robert taught him. She still had an hour to go before closing.

There were no customers in the store. Jazz went in the back. He saw her looking at the stock order form. Jazz said, "I'm glad you can make it." He was smiling at her.

She had a serious look on her face, but she quickly changed it to a smile as she got up and walked by him.

He said, "Where are you going?"

She said, "Nowhere." She got to the front door, grabbed an empty bag and a marker, and wrote "Closed for the Day. Family emergency." She got tape and stuck the sign on the door. Then she walked back to the office.

Jazz was watching her, but he had a question mark on his face, like, *Why are you closing early?*

She went back into the office, and he went in behind her. Sarah told him to count the stack of money over. The stack was five hundred- and twenty-dollar bills.

Jazz said, "It's all there."

She said, "Just count it over!"

He lifted the elastic off the bundle.

She said, "Sit down."

He was getting ready to say "Why," but before he was able to say it, she pulled out the gun. He yelled, "Sarah! What the fuck is wrong with you! Put the gun away."

Sarah said, "Fuck you. And I said sit down!"

Jazz could tell she knew how to use the gun. She had both hands on the powerful weapon. Robert taught her years ago how to shoot. Robert grew up in the country.

Patterson arrived back at the police station. He saw Durant going up the stairs and yelled, "Durant!"

Detective Durant turned around. He said, "How did it go?"

Patterson smiled at Durant and said, "Perfect." He also said, "I was wondering—could you accompany me in the arrest? I can get two uniforms if you can't do it." Patterson said, "I understand you got a list."

Detective Durant said, "You know I will go. Jazz, her houseguest, never got back to me, and it's been well over twenty-four hours. Now I'm going to arrest him if he's there as well. He will be only for questioning and as a potential suspect. I'll take my car."

Patterson said, "That's fine."

Detective Durant said, "If I get there before you, I will stand down till I see you, OK."

Detective Patterson said, "OK" and walked to his office to put up the compelling evidence of the weapon that Sarah used to murder Robert. After putting it away, he headed back out of the office. He walked to his unmarked car. Although it was late, he wanted to arrest her to ruin her evening. Detective Patterson was thinking of her husband. He didn't deserve to die. He was a good man.

He realized Detective Durant had already left.

Jazz said to Sarah, "I never stole no money from you or Robert."

She said, "It's not about you stealing money, you stupid ass!"

Jazz look puzzled as he stared in her eyes.

She said, "It's about my baby! Mikaela! You killed her!"

Jazz got scared. because now he knew she meant business. Jazz yelled, "I didn't kill Mikaela!"

Sarah yelled, "You did! And now you're going to die too!"

Jazz said, "You're making a big mistake to people you killed, Sarah! Really! Don't do this, Sarah!"

"Shut the fuck up," Sarah said. "You're going to die!"

Jazz said, "Why you had me count the money?"

She said, "'Cuz you was going to steal it. And I shot you in my store. They will believe me."

Jazz was getting mad because it sound good. He was black and a felon. He yelled at her, "Fuck you, Sarah!"

Sarah said, "Fuck you."

Detective Patterson headed to Sarah's home. Traffic was bad in the Square. He made a left to pass the heavy traffic. Traffic was much better, and as he was driving, he passed by the McKinley Hardware Store. He saw the store light was on, and Sarah's car was there. Detective Patterson also reflected on when he was working the night shift checking on the storefronts for burglaries. He realized that was decades ago. He needed to stop because Sarah should be home. Seeing her car at the store threw his arrest off a little. He parked his car, stepped out, and walked around Sarah's car. It looked OK. He started walking to the front of the door of the store. He heard muffled screams like an argument. It was two voices. He touched the front door. Ironically, it wasn't locked. He unholstered his weapon and crept inside the store. The voices were getting clearer. And one of the voices was very familiar to him.

The other voice he couldn't detect, but it was a male. He then realized the way the argument was going, it must be the guy they called Jazz. Detective Patterson was trying to listen and understand what they were arguing about. Patterson heard his heart in his ears. Even though he had been a policeman of over twenty-five years, the adrenaline rush still happens during tense situations. He quickly realized by the argument that Sarah has a weapon and was holding someone hostage, probably Jazz.

Patterson creeped closer to where they were. Sarah said, "Do you think I was going to let you get away with killing my daughter? You didn't like her anyways."

Jazz said, "You gotta believe me. I was only going to talk to her and see why she didn't like me."

Sarah told him, "Shut the fuck up, and look at me."

Jazz was facing her sideways. Patterson was near the door where they were arguing. He saw Sarah pointing the gun at Jazz. She had both hands on it, and she definitely meant business.

Patterson yelled, "Sarah, put down the gun!"

Sarah was startled, but she was still focused. She did not take her eyes off Jazz. Jazz was hoping she would because he would have lunged at her. He knew all he needed was a break. He was trying to talk to the detective, saying, "Thank God you're here."

Patterson told him to shut up. Patterson told Sarah to put down the gun.

She said, "Fuck you! He killed my daughter."

Jazz said, "That's a lie."

Patterson said, "Jazz, shut your fucking mouth."

Meanwhile, Detective Duran was sitting in front of the McKinley house. It had been a while, and still no Patterson. He felt uncomfortable and decided to pick up the radio and call his car number—8566 "Detective Patterson."

Detective Durant paused and waited for a response. Jazz, Sarah, and Patterson heard it. There was a moment's silence. Detective Durant said it again. "Detective Patterson, 8566, come on the air." Detective Durant said, "Detective Patterson, what's your location?"

Patterson said, "Sarah, put the gun down now. I don't want to shoot you. You've been through enough."

Sarah had tears in her eyes. She realized now that this was going to go bad.

Jazz was getting more confident to leap on Sarah. He was just thinking he needed one more distraction to throw her in a pause-and-delay effect.

Detective Patterson said, "Jazz will be prosecuted, I promise you."

Sarah said, "No, he'll get off. My daughter is fucking dead because of him, and he is going to pay."

Detective Durant was getting worried. He made one more attempt to get Detective Patterson to respond. He said, "Detective Patterson, come on the air."

Patterson looked at Sarah and Jazz and then back at Sarah. He was still holding his weapon on Sarah. With his left hand, he pressed the button down. Detective Patterson said, "8566.1013."

On 1825 West Main Street, Detective Durant heard it. He screeched from Sarah's residence. Durant realized that the address was the hardware store. It also meant officer in distress, and it was Patterson. Jazz knew this was going to go bad, and he would do a lot of time way more than before. In his mind, he was never going back.

Patterson said, "Sarah, please put the gun down. Everyone's coming. I don't want this to end bad."

She said, "Jazz is a bad man. He killed my daughter."

Patterson said, "I know this."

Jazz said, "Bullshit."

Patterson said, "Jazz, I'm not telling you to shut your mouth no more."

Jazz was losing patience and was now willing to take the risk.

Detective Durant yelled, "Patterson! Where are you! I am here! Backup is coming too."

Sarah looked at Detective Patterson.

Jazz leap at her. He thought he had her reach mapped out, but she stepped back out of his reach.

She fired a single shot and struck Jazz in the forehead; and before she realized it, the bullet had killed him. She turned to Detective Patterson pointing the gun, but she had no intention of shooting him; it was just out of response and her movement of turning to him.

Detective Patterson fired a shot, striking her in the shoulder. She dropped the gun. Patterson had his weapon pointed at her. He watched her every move until he got to her weapon. He was ready to fire another round if he needed to. He pressed his radio: "Shots fired in 1825 West Main Street, two people hit and in critical condition. I need EMS."

Durant was yelling, "Patterson! Patterson!" as he made his way back to the store office.

Patterson said, "I'm OK, I'm OK."

Durant scanned the room. He asked Patterson, "Is there anyone else?"

Patterson said, "No, just those two." As Patterson was handcuffing Sarah, he told Detective Durant, "This is Jazz—the one you wanted to interview."

Detective Durant walked near him, and he said, "I guess he can't tell me anything now. He is dead."

Detective Patterson said, "I heard Sarah arguing with him."

Sarah said, "Yes, he killed my daughter. I killed him."

Detective Patterson said, "Yes, and you also killed Robert, your husband. Sarah, you are under arrest for the murder of Robert McKinley and Jazz St. Jean. You have the right to remain silent . . ."

As Detective Patterson was reading her her rights, you could hear the blaring of the sirens as EMTs and police cars were approaching the scene.

The EMS team was yelling, "Is anyone hurt?"

Durant said, "Yeah, back here."

One started working on Sarah. The other one checked out Jazz, who he came to the conclusion was deceased.

Detective Patterson called the coroner's office and let them know they needed to come to 1825 West Main Street.

Sarah was handcuffed and put in the ambulance. Detective Patterson rode in the back, and Durant followed the ambulance.

As everyone pulled away, Sarah's life would never be the same. Caitlin would be raised by Robert McKinley's sister. She would go to school in their area.

Sarah was found guilty for the murders of Robert McKinley and Jazz St. Jean and was sentenced to eighteen to twenty-five years for both murders. She would be serving her sentences concurrently.

CPSIA information can be obtained
at www.ICGtesting.com
Printed in the USA
BVHW030313231119
564632BV00002B/118/P